Call Me Guido

Mike Fiorito

Praise for Call Me Guido

"The memoir and music in Michael Fiorito's *Call Me Guido* are "drenched in the world time has left behind." Fiorito's embrace of music is an act of love and completion. 'I don't want to like my father's music,' he writes. Yet, it's the songs of Sinatra, Bennett, Roselli that bring to life the Italian-American experience—an experience that can't be unwound from the ancient music of Italy brought to this country on the backs of immigrants. Fiorito's writing traces not only the father-son story but the story of the beating heart of music in America; this is an Italian rhythm and style, 'bel canto … it is vulnerable, but it is strong.'"

-- Jennifer Martelli, author of *My Tarantella*

"Mike Fiorito navigates his readers through the ethnic twilight of the 21st century Italian-American experience in Call Me Guido, a book that is hilarious, thought-provoking, and poignant in equal measure. Fiorito's Call Me Guido will be regarded as a seminal work of Italian-American literature."

-- Alfonso Colasuonno, cofounder of *Beautiful Losers Magazine*

"Mike Fiorito's *Call Me Guido*, is a poignant, sometimes painful, often hilarious collection of stories about growing up Italian in Queens, New York. It's filled with rich dialogue and recollections of family interactions that carry us below the surface, and surprises we can't help but love, like his tale 'Because of You', about his odd Uncle Tutti, who turns out to be the superstar Tony Bennett, or his hard working mother, 'a tribe, a history of her family', and of course his father, a gambler, opinionated, historian, and a complex mix that makes a relationship of father and son seem totally impossible to characterize, and yet Michael does, captivating us all along the way. I love this book!"

-- Louisa Calio, author of *Journey to the Heart Waters*

"Mike Fiorito's stories start quietly, gently pulling the reader in through compelling dialogue and scene setting and then erupting into slices of life many of us can relate to or that let us peek into the lives of others. This collection, in quick bites, informs, entertains, and surprises---a masterpiece of storytelling."

-- John Keahey, author of *Seeking Sicily*

Mike Fiorito

Call Me Guido

Ovunque Siamo Press

Ambler, PA

Produced in the United States of America

ISBN-13: 978-1-7339948-0-4

Dedicated with love to my mother and father.

Table of Contents

Call Me Guido

Foreword
by Paul Paolicelli

Luigi and I were visiting a lake on the outskirts of Rome one sunny Sunday afternoon. A vendor was selling Lupini beans at a small concession stand on the lake's edge. I happily purchased a paper cone filled with the treats, remembering my cousin Frankie and our mutual love of the same.

"You know what these are?" asked an astonished Luigi. "No, you can't know these, these are not American."

"No, they're not American," I replied. "They're definitely Italian. You forget, so am I."

I happily munched away. Luigi looked incredulous.

Luigi had a tough time accepting my heritage. I was the epitome of an American as far as he was concerned. Being both Italian and American just didn't compute in his mind, nor did it add up for most Italians of my acquaintance during my three-year sojourn in Italy. Knowledge of Lupini beans weren't supposed to be in my range. Romans didn't recognize the hyphen, or had a hard time understanding why any of us felt a linkage to a culture in which we hadn't been born or raised.

It's always amazed me that when many of the Italian-American groups want to set up a cultural outreach, the first thing they do (after the interminable and obvious cooking classes) is offer Italian language training. I have no objections to anyone learning that lovely language, but I quickly point out that Italian-Americans of my generation mostly don't speak Italian and that there are some very important historical reasons for that lack of language. More importantly, that the Italian language isn't necessary in understanding our unique culture. Italians don't consider us Italians. And they consider the language that our grandparents and great-grandparents brought with them to the United States to be inferior, base, vulgar and, to use their word, *brutta*—ugly.

In other words, we're a totally separate culture. A culture born in Italy but raised in America. We kept some, but not all, of our Italian parts and have many more purely American elements in our nature. It's only been within the past twenty-five years or so that we've begun the analysis of that linkage in our contemporary literature. Many of us have attempted articles and books to evaluate the lasting legacy that we've been given. We're the last generation to have direct links to the great immigration wave of 1880-1920. And the influence of those hearty pioneers remains in our veins, though they are all gone now and most of their children have also departed. What my generation is left with is memories of long-ago Sunday dinners hearing marvelous accents, fascinating stories and ironic insights. We have also spent our lives with a sensibility that we now realize is that thing we call "Italian" but in truth is fully Italian-American.

Mike Fiorito is one of those analysts. He hears his heritage in the songs wafting out into the street from the neighborhood tavern. He senses his father in his everyday outlook. He understands the nature of our very separate and very distinct culture. And he writes joyously of the same. It's the "Italian" singers that spark Mike's imagination, but can you imagine an America without Sinatra or Bennett or Como or Martin? They're the perfect synthesis of our cultures; pure Americana with Marinara sauce. A delightful and exotic mixture that has enriched the American society with Italian sensibilities.

My nickname has been "Guido" for a very long time now; a name that only those closest to me ever use. So you can call me Guido too. And hopefully find in this lovely little book the music of our uniquely Italian-American song.

Preface

About twelve years ago, walking down Columbia Street in Carroll Gardens, Brooklyn, where I then lived, I heard music coming from a restaurant. At the time, Carroll Gardens was still a very Italian-American neighborhood with numerous Italian restaurants dotting the sidewalks. Sometimes, you'd hear and see patrons singing songs with a live band, or with karaoke music. On this night, I peered in the window having heard a voice streaming into the street. The singer was an amateur, accompanied by a backing track. He was dressed in a shiny polyester suit. Watching that man sing sparked a journey of rediscovery of my family that was slipping away. It was at that moment that "Call Me Guido" was born.

"Call Me Guido" is about three generations of Italian-American father-and-son relationships. The stories focus on the relationships of the characters, but are connected through themes of Italian-American singers, like Frank Sinatra, Jimmy Roselli and Tony Bennett. Each story could be read independently. In fact, many of the stories have been published serially, but when read as a collection, there is an arc of resolution and return.

Simultaneously confronting and courting Italian-American stereotypes head-on, all of the stories are connected by crooner themes: an uncle who discovers himself by believing he's Tony Bennett; a son discovering Sinatra's fragility while driving with his father; Bobby Darin selling his soul to possess the gift of performance; a mother, dark and strong, like the earth itself, teaching her son the meaning of strength; a mobster hired to kill a singer who wouldn't kowtow to the mob.

Most of the stories are written from the perspective of a son making sense of his family's Italian-American past. Now a father himself, the son tries to make peace with the trauma inflicted on his family by his father's gambling addiction. Despite the fact that the father's debt cast his family into a place where everything was out of reach, the main character discovers the strength and richness of his Italian-American heritage. There are gamblers and mobsters, but philosophers and poets too.

In these sometimes gritty depictions of hard times, there are many tender and comic moments. The soundtrack to these tender moments is the music of the crooners.

One More for My Dad

Driving in the car with my father, he reaches over to turn on the radio, steering with his left hand. He puts on "The Imaginary Ballroom," a program that plays Sinatra, Martin and Bennett.

Sinatra's voice emerges warmly from the speakers.

"Yes, it's alright with me," Sinatra sings sweetly. The song is not full of bravado; it's tender and hesitant. He's telling a woman that she looks like his previous lover; she has sweet lips too, like his old lover. He says that if she's lonely one night, it's alright if she kisses him with those lips.

We never hear her response.

I hate to admit that it's a great song and that Sinatra sings it dramatically and convincingly. I don't want to like my father's music — he desperately wants me to.

I look over at my dad; he turns the music up louder.

There are parts of the song that Sinatra sings in a whisper. He's pleading with the woman. This is not the Sinatra I had despised growing up. A braggart, a "wop" gangster. This is the voice of a fragile and sensitive person. If I said this to my father, he'd say, "You're too deep for me," which would piss me off. I'd hear that as "I don't want to talk about that kind of shit with you." So I don't say anything. I have a reputation to uphold with my dad. I am the tough, independent kid, unlike my brother Frank who, as a kid, cried when my mother washed his hair in the tub.

I am also the one who punched a kid in the face so hard when I was about eight or nine, I knocked his tooth out. The kid's father was so angry he came to our house, knocked on the door.

My father opened the door.

"Do you know your son punched my son in the mouth and knocked his tooth out?"

My father looked at the kid. He had a big gap to the left of his two front teeth.

"I want your son to apologize," the other man said.

"Michael," my father shouted, "please come here."

I came to the door, dirt still on my face from playing outside.

The man looked me up and down then looked at his own son. Standing next to his kid, I was about a head shorter.

"You let this kid knock your teeth out?" the man asked his son, fixing his stare at me.

His son started to cry, like he was about to get a worse beating than the one I'd given him.

The man grabbed his son by the shirt, and dragged him away.

When they were gone, my dad said, "You gotta learn to control yourself." He didn't yell at me. He never directly encouraged me to fight, but when retelling the story to my mom at the dinner table, he laughed a bit.

"He don't take shit from no one, this kid," he said. Being tough might get me far. The world is cruel.

Then, when I was about fourteen, he and my mom came back from a parent-teacher meeting at my school.

"I met Mr. Amato," my father said. Mr. Amato was my science teacher. It was his first year and my classmates and I weren't interested in making it easy on him. In the lab, I had hit a kid in the back of the head with a frog kidney.

"He said he has a hard time keeping the class in order."

I listened attentively, curious to hear what else Mr. Amato had to say.

"I raised my hand," my father said, "and asked him if he could single out the troublemakers and punish them." I told him I thought that was a good idea.

"He asked me my last name," my father said, then paused.

"When I told him Fiorito, you know what he said?"

"I don't know," I said.

"He said, your son," – my father paused and sighed – "is the ringleader of the group."

He looked disapprovingly at me, curling his tongue in his cheek.

"Ringleader" echoed in my head over and over.

Shaking his head, he had a slight grin on his face. He seemed to at least be proud that I was in charge.

The sound of the Sinatra songs brings me back to the present.

We stop at a red light; my father taps his fingers on the steering wheel and then looks over at me.

He lowers the music.

"Why do you have a mopey face on?" he asks.

"No reason." I'm not sure what in particular was bothering me, but I'm sure something was. Something was always bothering me.

"Are you worried about us going to live with grandma?"

I'm not, but I say yes. The housing authority had found out that my mom was working and had evicted us from the projects. Since rent was based on income, we were at fault for not declaring my mother's earnings. But my mother paid the rent; my father's gambling debt consumed almost all of the income he made. Whereas my father was a gambler, sometimes stripped into vulnerability, my mother was constant, hardworking and indefatigable.

"Don't worry, everything will be okay."

I am not worried about that, at least I don't think I am.

"We'll be there for only a few months," he says.

"Grandma lives near your school," he adds.

I think of how nice it will be to walk to school, instead of taking two buses every morning.

He turns up the music again.

I change the station, looking at him for approval.

He nods okay.

"I Can't Get No Satisfaction" is playing.

My father lowers the music.

"I like this song," I say over Jagger's shrieking "And I try, and I try."

"It's noisy," he says. "This is the guy who struts like a rooster?"

He starts to jerk his head back and forth, mimicking Jagger.

I make a face at him. "He does more than dance like a rooster," I say.

I hear Jagger's words about not wanting to listen to TV announcers and wanting to do his own thing as if he is speaking to me directly.

I don't know if my father hears the words, or if they would matter to him. Jagger is a rooster, is all he knows.

"He's alright," my father says. "He's got balls. Can't sing, but he's got balls."

You don't know shit about music, I think to myself.

I look out the window.

I'm thinking about Mick Jagger and then about how Maria Hermano sucked my dick earlier that day.

"I told you not to worry," my father says. "It's going to be okay."

I'm happy he's worried about me, even if for the wrong reasons.

"We're going to stop over at Pete's to get sausage," he says, "before we pick up Mom at the train station."

I nod.

"Satisfaction" is over. He looks at me before turning the station back to the oldies.

"Old Devil Moon," sung by Tony Bennett, comes on.

He looks at me, raising the volume.

"It's not noisy; this is quiet music."

The guitar playing is terrific. Bennett's vocals swing with feeling.

"You like this?"

I shrug my shoulders, saying, "I don't know."

"Is he the one that looks like a parrot?" I ask to get him back for the knock on Jagger.

"What, Bennett?"

I point to the radio.

He's got a big Italian nose, like my father.

"He sings like a parrot."

"At least he doesn't strut like a rooster."

We both laugh a little, but I don't reply. I let him get the last word so I can hear the rest of the song.

Because of You

Making a big entrance, Uncle Tutti arrived late at my high-school graduation party, like a Hollywood star. He wore a smart black suit, bone-white tie and black and white checkered Domino shoes.

"My godson," said Uncle Tutti, pinching my cheek with his thumb and index finger, slyly handing me an envelope with the other.

"Now, I'm going to sing you a song," he said.

Tutti pulled away from me, his periwinkle blue eyes sparkling like precious stones.

Then, turning his back to us, Tutti began speaking to the musicians, giving instructions. Tutti adjusted his suit, giving his white-gold pinky ring a twist, making sure the sapphire stone faced forward.

He then turned around, looked toward me and said "this is for you kid. I love you." He threw a kiss toward me. I turned red and laughed nervously. I was on stage too.

The band broke out with a romping intro. Tutti spun around, his hands out, fingers splayed and sang "Rags to Riches."

Like a man possessed, his eyes were wide open and red with fire. As he thrust his hands in the air, shaking them, spit sprayed from his mouth. With each rhythmic stop, he clapped his hands together and stomped his foot, right in step with the band.

My father shouted, "Sing it, Tutti!" as he applauded his younger brother.

Only recently, my father told me that when Tutti was younger he'd been depressed and confused. "He seemed lost in the world," my father said. "I introduced him to my friends, tried to get him a girlfriend."

There was a time, my father said, when Tutti believed himself to be the Emperor of The Kingdom of the Two Sicilies. Who knew there was an emperor of Sicily? Two Sicilies?

He memorized the writing of medieval Sicilian poets which he performed at weddings, funerals, and confirmations. The performances were tolerated.

As the Emperor, he'd taken to wearing vests and fake ruby rings. Since these poems were meant to be sung, he sang them.

In other words, everyone thought Tutti was crazy.

At one Christmas party he showed up wearing his colorful costume and sang his songs. My grandmother said to my father, "*Lui è pazzo*, I wish he could be more like you, *figlio mio. Normale.* He's crazy. I don't know what's in his head."

My grandmother cried, making the sign of the cross, kissing the Saint Anthony pendant on her neck.

"What have I done to offend God that one of my sons is a *meschino*?" she asked. She once put a Saint Anthony statue on the window sill in the rain for weeks; this was her way of protesting to the saint about her son's craziness.

My father didn't say anything. Tutti didn't mean to hurt anybody. At least being the Emperor of the Two Sicilies seemed to chase away Tutti's despair. My father remembered Tutti as the little kid who played alone in the schoolyard, the teenager who didn't have any friends.

And my grandfather didn't know what to make of Tutti either. His bizarre and fine manner of dress and speech were *uno coso pazzo*, a crazy thing. "He's a little too much, no?" my grandfather asked. "It's because he works in that flower store," said grandpa. Grandpa had worked in mines; he knew how to hammer stone, how to break rocks in the glare of the sun. What did he know about a flower shop?

Then one night at Tomasino's restaurant in Carroll Gardens, Brooklyn, Uncle Tutti became Tony Bennett.

It was a sudden and profound transformation.

Patrons particularly liked Tomasino's because they could sing a song or two with the band; it was encouraged. Everyone had an uncle, a brother, a father, a cousin, or a friend who could sing, who would sing. Sometimes you'd hear a voice that could stop you in your tracks, make you put down your fork and listen. Sometimes you'd hear a note so flat it would cut through your brain like an icepick.

Unsuspectingly, Uncle Tutti got up and headed for the bandstand during dinner this time. No one had ever heard him sing these kinds of songs before. No one knew he could sing these songs. He walked up to the stage slowly. His shoulders were slumped. He wore a plain black suit and regular black shoes.

He wrestled with the microphone, pulling it off of the stand. Being too close to the speakers, there was a sudden shriek of feedback. A high frequency scream cut through the dark room like a howling demon, making some faces wince.

We all expected him to be terrible. My father looked at me nervously. Tutti was going to embarrass himself. My grandmother made the sign of the cross. I wondered what she might do to the Saint Anthony statue this time.

Then, barely holding himself up in the spotlight, he began to sing "Because of You."

The first words came out weak and strained. Eyes were rolling. People shook their heads knowingly.

Then, to the astonishment of everyone, he stood up straight and tall. He began to sweep his right arm out, as if pushing out the notes, as he sang. His voice hit the back of the room like a freight train.

Suddenly, all of the talking stopped. The old men with thick boxy glasses and gold teeth, who had been speaking frantically with their hands, turned to look at the stage. The women with beehive hairdos and gold crosses hushed. He sang powerfully, as if killer mastiffs were at his side and he was declaring himself dictator of the world.

When Tutti changed into Tony Bennett, he became more like everyone else. He sang songs everyone knew and loved. People would say *canta una canzone*, sing a song, Tutti. My grandmother believed that she had finally cast off his spell. The *malocchio* pendants that hung in the kitchen, in the bedroom, over the doors, had chased away the demons from Tutti.

Finally, my grandfather decided Tutti had virtues after all. "He always had a way with the girls at that flower shop," Grandpa said. "No?" he asked.

Hidden in Lights

A few weeks ago, my eighty-two year old mother, Cookie, fell face first into the wall at home, seriously wounding her collarbone. She didn't tell anyone. Days later my sister, Patty, saw the purpled bruise streaking down from her shoulder and across her chest.

"What's this?" Patty said, lifting the part of Cookie's shirt that covered the bruise.

"It's nothing."

"Nothing? Mom, please, tell me what happened," pleaded Patty, out of her mind with worry.

Cornered into telling the truth, Cookie confessed.

At this point, we're not really sure whether or not Cookie even wants to live. My sisters, brother, and I take turns calling her, visiting her, taking her out, taking her away. Anytime we see her could be the last time.

I call to ask if she wants to go away for Labor Day.

"Do you want to go the beach at Montauk?" I ask. "They still have available rooms," I add, knowing she probably doesn't want to go.

She's silent.

"Mom?"

"I don't think so," she says. In Montauk she'd be stuck peering out at the world from the keyhole of a hotel room. As it is, she's home almost every day, still working one day a week. Work is her last grip on the outside world. She is at war with the seasons. Her unsteady feet can slip on the ice. The summer promises skies of hell flames.

"Do you think we can book something at Atlantic City?"

I'm nauseous just imagining the melody of slot machines, noise, and smoke. With Labor Day only a few days away, I doubt that we'll be able to book a room for all of us.

"Let me see if I can get a complimentary room," says my mom, coughing into the phone. She knows all of the reps at the Tropicana. They give her free lodging in return for the money she spends at the tables. Before she hangs up I hear the clinking of ice in her glass.

The next day Cookie calls me. Not only has she received a complimentary two night stay with two beds, the Tropicana offers her dinner for four at PF Chang's.

On the way to Atlantic City, Cookie is quiet, sitting in the back seat next to my son, Desi.

"Are you okay back there?" I ask, looking at her in the rearview mirror. Her eyes are four times their normal size behind the lenses of her glasses.

My wife, Bea, tries to talk to her, turning around in her seat. Cookie doesn't talk back much. This isn't like her.

"Stop for a cigarette?" I ask, after driving about one hour into New Jersey. I know her nerves are rattled from not smoking.

Stepping out of the car, the scorching September sun pours on my face, heavy and thick like lava. I can smell the burning tires from the highway.

My mother swings the car door open on her side before I can open it for her. The door smacks back on her. Normally this wouldn't matter. But in her case, her bones weakening, more brittle every day, the door is a weapon. I should have rushed to open it. I can hear my brother's panicked voice in my head, "that's why you need to get the door for her." Frank follows her around, nervously, like a madcap butler, holding her arm, helping her. "I'll do it myself," Cookie shouts at him. He ignores her shouts and never lets her go.

Back in the car, Cookie says that the door left a black and blue mark on her ankle. We have to be prepared for anything.

Driving in on the narrow road that leads to Atlantic City, I can see the shiny golden buildings and glittering facades. The skyline looks like a heap of costume jewelry.

Checking in at the Tropicana, I get a first glimpse inside of Atlantic City. There's a husband and wife on line arguing.

"What the hell do you want from me?" the husband shrieks. "I told them I don't got no more money for them to come."

"They're my cousins," his wife says. She has a red beehive hairdo. An oversized gold cross hangs from her neck. "You said you was gonna invite them."

The husband grumbles. As I scan the hotel lobby, it reminds me of the Off Track Betting places my father took me to as a child. Like at the OTB, the faces of the people at the Tropicana sweat with worry. Their worn clothes, two decades out of fashion, look saggy and defeated. I am reminded of all of the old worries about my father's gambling. My parents' anxiety about not having enough money to pay the rent. Being sent to the auditorium with the other school kids whose parents didn't pay tuition. Knocks on our apartment door from people in long coats, their faces hidden under hats. My mother haranguing my already beaten down father. Night after night.

"Smoking or non-smoking?" the hotel clerk asks.

"Non-smoking, please," I answer.

"Sonofabitch," my mother says. "You're such a phony. I can't believe you."

"Please Mom. I can't breathe in a smoking room."

"No one smoked like you."

"That was thirty years ago." She's never forgiven me for quitting. "What about Desi?" She doesn't respond.

Cookie takes the access card and gives it to me, her hands shaky and tense. I fight back my guilt, knowing I'll never get a wink of sleep in a smoking room.

We head to the room to drop off our luggage. I hold my mother's arm and warily guide her through the corridors of the hotel.

Patty had told me to drop my mother at the casino then head to the beach. "You can pick her up later," Patty said. "If you left her in the casino for a week straight she'd be fine. You come back and she'd still be there smoking a cigarette, drinking a scotch." I don't like the idea of dropping her off at the casino. It's like I'm dropping off my child with a psychotic babysitter.

Unlike me, Bea doesn't nitpick about my mother's edginess, or about mine either. She guides us to the casino, knowing I will only get us lost.

"Take me to the Wheel of Fortune," my mother says. "That's where the action is." We walk deeper into the casino, passing a lady with gold teeth carrying a bag that looks like it contains everything she owns. A man sucks on his cigarette, his eyes rheumy and swollen. He looks like he hasn't slept, like he drinks until his liver gushes with blood every night.

"Not here," my mother says.

I don't like anything about this place. I can't breathe. My heart feels knotted. There is a constant din of noise. Amongst the jingles and rings of the casino machines there are screams coming from the people as they win or lose, outcries of woe, loud moans. I am trapped inside a deranged arcade, blinded by the flashing multicolored lights and assaulted by the deafening ringing of the slot machines. Hopefully a cliff will appear out of nowhere that I can fall off of, hurtling to my death.

We keep walking into rooms nested in still other rooms. When we finally find the Wheel of Fortune, my lungs feel like rusty engine parts from the smoke.

"This is it," my mother says, pointing to the machine. We walked all this way and it looks like all of the others.

I help Cookie sit down next to a woman drinking scotch from a plastic cup. The woman's eyes spin with wheeling flames, reflecting the wheels on the slot machine. One seat over, a man with one eye open pulls the slot handle without looking at the machine.

There are cigarettes squashed in ashtrays, rows of bottles, and near empty plastic cups, some filled with cigarette butts.

"Are you sure?" I ask my mother, thinking I am leaving her in a miserable ditch of hell. I am dizzy from the lack of oxygen, the blaring sounds and flashing lights.

"This is perfect," she says. "Go to the beach. I'm fine."

I stay, waiting for her to start playing. Bea doesn't rush, either. She's strong like my mother. She takes all of this in stride, looking at me to see if I'm upset. She's managing everyone's terrors in her soundless way.

A waitress comes to take my mother's drink order. The waitress is an older lady herself. After writing down the order, she hobbles away in her high-heeled shoes, hardly able to walk.

"Go already," Cookie barks suddenly. Then softly, "It's nice out and you'll enjoy the beach."

Bea and I linger.

"I said go," she says, sternly now.

Bea nods at me, motioning to leave. Desi trails behind us. The last thing I see is the back of Cookie's little head.

"I'm shocked," I say to Bea.

"I can imagine," she says.

"After all we went through with my father's gambling," I say, "and she wants to gamble."

"She likes to gamble. It makes her happy," says Bea. "This is Cookie's heaven and your hell. The smoking I can do without."

"I hate the smoking."

Later that night, at PF Chang's, we're having drinks. Desi hides under the table. I can't see him, but it bothers me that he's probably crawling in piles of greasy fried rice and sticky puddles of soda.

Cookie is smiling. The drinks, smoking, and gambling have calmed her. Looking at the menu, she says, "I'll order. I know what to get and I want to have a taste of everything."

It's easier if Bea and I just agree.

Cookie tells Bea that she started going to casinos in the Bahamas when my grandmother was dying of cancer. They went to an alternative cancer center in Freeport. That's where Cookie started drinking and gambling. Now, holding Bea's hand, my mother recalls her own mother.

"She was a special woman. Never one to complain. And good to the core. Right?" she gestures towards me.

"She was like a Gandhi," I say, half-jokingly.

"I don't know about that," my mother says. "She was giving and kind. And when she got sick … I'm going to cry now." She pauses, takes a breath. "When she got sick, I couldn't let go," she says, swallowing her words.

I reach out and hold Cookie's hand. She doesn't cry easily.

"I couldn't let her die." Her words weigh down on us. Now sitting on my lap, Desi rocks back and forth, playing with my glasses.

"I couldn't let her die, not so much for her," she repeats, wiping teardrops from her eyes, "but for me." Now we are all crying. The release is like a downpour after a hot day.

After dinner, we walk my mother back to the casino. Bea takes us back to the Wheel of Fortune where Cookie finds her lucky machine. An overweight woman is sitting next to my mother's machine, breathing out of the folds of her neck. The woman smiles as we approach. She's enveloped in a cloud of smoke.

I help Cookie sit down. She immediately lights a cigarette, blowing the smoke in my face. Desi starts banging on the machine, pressing buttons randomly. Immediately, guards rush over to us.

"Children aren't allowed to play the machines," one of the guards says, talking into his walkie-talkie, rushing at us. Another guard hurries towards us. I don't know what's happening. Knocking the fire from her cigarette, my mother says it's not legal for kids to even touch the machines.

"I hate this place," Desi whines. "There are no games for children." He can only look at the blinking lights. It's like an amusement park with rides he can't go on.

"We'll pick you up a little later," I shout to my mother over my shoulder as we're escorted out by the casino police.

Bea, Desi, and I escape to the boardwalk. It's a cool night. The air feels fresh, especially after fleeing the haze of the casino. There are electronic billboards displaying ads and music videos. Even the outside rings with its own din.

Bea and I know we have to do something for little Desi. He's been locked in cars and hotel rooms. We take him to a video arcade. He pounces on a car racing video machine, punching the controls, wildly spinning the wheel. Desi smashes into other cars, drives off of cliffs into bodies of water. He thinks the point of the game is to get into accidents and drive off the road. Bea and I laugh until tears run down our faces.

A few hours later, Bea and Desi head up to the room and I go in search of The Wheel of Fortune to get my mom. I'm lost walking through a maze, blinded by the alternating lights and smoke. For a moment I feel panic. I'll never find her. Every slot machine looks the same. I see the people gambling, as if with their last dollars, maybe some have sold valuable possessions to keep playing. This looks like the waiting room for the dying.

I finally find Cookie sitting next to a man with a cane. His hair is wispy and gray. His eyes, fierce and strange, are covered with cataracts. He is blind. How is he playing?

My mom doesn't notice me. She is in the innermost core of the casino. In her left hand she holds a scotch in a plastic cup. With her right hand, she pulls the lever on The Wheel of Fortune. The slot machine now shimmers like an altar, its brassy surface glittering and fiery.

Through the dense smoke, I see a squadron of angels girdle her majestic seat. My mother has said that time slips away when she gambles. When she pulls the handle, she is plunged back in time. Cookie is now thirty years old and with my father again. Her face is smooth, her hair is dark black. She and my father are on vacation in Florida. Now she is pregnant with my older sister; her lips cherry red, her brown eyes on fire with life. Now Cookie is by my father's side in the hospital. He is dying. The hole that my father burned into my mother's soul with the pain of his gambling has become the vehicle through which she can now visit him.

Suddenly, the smoke from the cigarettes balls up in my lungs and explodes. I cough.

The scene comes to an abrupt halt. I have disturbed the magical forces at play.

"Hi Mom, having fun?" I say, now standing over her, my hand over my mouth to hide my gagging.

She points to the cards on the screen.

"Nothing, see?"

I don't really follow the game. I don't know three card rummy or poker or any card game really besides solitaire. I am drawn to Tarot cards. The Fool. The Magician. The Hermit. The Hangman. I prefer magicians, shamans, and gypsies to gamblers. Maybe they're all gamblers anyway.

My mother presses the button to refresh her hand.

"Nothing again."

I can tell she's had too much to drink.

"So are you ready to come up?"

"In a little while," she says.

"Have you won?"

"Not tonight."

She resumes pressing the button, dealing her a new hand. She keeps losing.

As I look around I see a light shimmering from a gigantic chandelier over the casino. It feels warm, penetrating the freezing air conditioning.

When she's ready to leave, I lift her up. There's no way she could have walked back to the room in this condition. This woman is like a mountain. She is stubborn and powerful, with marshy soft parts and deep dark caverns. Everyone has died around her. She holds onto life with a grip that both whitens her knuckles and rattles her knees. She hates winter and summer and in turn they are fearful of her. They lie waiting for her to stumble.

When I help Cookie stand up, she is drenched with the world that has left her behind. She is a tribe, a history of her family, fiercely clinging to this world. She is heavy in my arms. It feels as if I am lifting a piece of the earth, earth inhabited by a race of people. This is not just any little old lady.

Call Me Guido

When I was a kid, my father played Jimmy Roselli and other Neapolitan singers for me. Back then I hated it. He took me to the Italian novelty store, E. Rossi & Company, on Grand Street in Little Italy as if to impress me with the Neapolitan music they played. It was too Italian for me. Too narrow. I wanted to see the world, not be imprisoned in our family heritage or a national identity.

Twenty-five years later, I've amassed a collection of recordings of the Neapolitan singers and read many books and articles on the subject. Now, I go down to E. Rossi & Company to play guitar with Ernie, the owner. I look through his record collection, searching for a Neapolitan singer I don't know or an album I don't have.

The fact is I've become obsessed with the topic. I'm searching for more than information. I'm resurrecting my father. I'm communicating with him across time and place. When I write these pieces, I'm writing them for him first. To delight him. To share my enthusiasm with him. I know my father would have loved to read them.

When I learned that the first six-stringed guitar is said to have been made in Naples, I wished I could have visited him. The conversation may have gone something like this.

"I have some interesting news for you, Dad."

"I'm listening," he'd say, not yet looking up from his crossword puzzle, tapping his foot, snug in a slipper, on the floor.

"Have you heard of Giovanni Battista Fabricatore?"

"I may be dead, but I'm not stupid."

"Fabricatore, a Neapolitan luthier, made the first six-stringed guitar," I'd say, proud to have discovered this fact. To share it with him.

"Listen kid, I always told you the Italians were the first in many things. And especially the Neapolitans. Do I have to give you a list of our accomplishments?" he'd say sternly, then smile. The joke was always a breath away with my father.

"You know I'm learning this stuff for you?"

He'd stop being facetious now, his face would soften and his bright eyes would suddenly beam.

"You know I'm busting your chops. This is just like you. You become obsessed about things. It's one of your strengths. To be honest, it drove me nuts sometimes." He'd see that I had taken a little offense to what he'd just said. Then he'd add, "But it doesn't now."

And he would tell everyone else, when I wasn't around, what I was writing about. He'd bring copies of my books, essays, and stories around with him wherever he went.

My father's teasing was his way of saying he liked you. If he teased you, it meant he felt you could take it. I saw him do it with only some of my friends. It was an honor that he bestowed on you. The difference with me is that I teased him back. We poked at each other. The joking was mixed with honest criticism. It was never bitter. It never went too far.

To tease me, my father told me that he wanted to name me Guido when I was a kid. Guido would have been the worst name possible for a kid from Queens. A Guido was a guy who talked funny, wore gaudy clothes and drove a Camaro. This was the entire point.

"I love the name Guido," he said.

"It's stupid, I hate the name Guido," I replied.

"Why, it's a great name. You should be proud of it. It's Italian."

"A Guido is a guy who slicks his hair and wears white shoes."

But some of the greatest Italians were Guidos. Among them was Guido d'Arezzo, who invented modern musical notation in approximately 1025. Guido Arezzo wrote "Micrologus," a guide that helped singers learn and remember Gregorian chants. "Micrologus" is considered the second most widely read medieval treatise in Europe after the writings of Boethius.

In the 18th century, the control of territories and regions passed between the hands of kings. Naples was under the rule of the Spanish king. And being devout Catholics, the Spanish monarchs opened music conservatories to teach church music to young children. If nothing else, the church was always a patron of the arts. Spanish control of Naples, however, was short lived. In 1806, Napoleon marched into Naples, claiming it as his own. Napoleon's rule opened conservatories to commercial interests; composers now wrote concertos and compositions in his honor. And despite the turmoil that Napoleon created, music remained central to the culture of Naples. Perhaps because Naples was the stomping ground of multiple nations, it acquired various influences. It is said that Neapolitan music developed a light melodic quality. The Neapolitan dialect became a signature of musical styles in the rest of Europe.

Another interesting development at this time, specifically in Naples, was the emergence of the guitar as a serious instrument.

With kingdoms and courts came the appetite and the resources for cultural and artistic development. There was an explosion of music conservatories in Naples. And this profusion of major music conservatories drove an industry of instrument production techniques in Naples as well. The making of stringed or bowed instruments, such as the violin, the cello, the mandolin and the guitar, flourished in and around Naples. In addition to Fabricatore, there were other well-known luthiers of the 18th and 19th centuries in Naples, such as Vinaccia, Filano, Calace, and Alessandro Gagliano. Gagliano was an apprentice of Antonio Stradivari in Cremona and was largely responsible for transitioning violin making to Naples.

Some of the Neapolitan guitar makers migrated to America, bringing centuries of luthier traditions with them. Among these was John D'Angelico, who opened D'Angelico Guitars in Little Italy in 1932. D'Angelico used the same techniques he learned from his uncle, an expert violin and mandolin maker, to design and build some of the most beautiful guitars the world has ever known. In 1952, D'Angelico then apprenticed Jimmy D'Aquisto in his shop. Some consider D'Aquisto to be the greatest electric-guitar maker that ever lived. Thus, the lineage of guitar making can be drawn directly from Cremona, to Naples, and on to New York City's Little Italy.

And then there were a number of Italian guitar players who would have been influenced by the Neapolitan composers, players, and luthiers who shaped the legacy of the instrument.

Although better known as a violin player, Paganini was said to be a dazzling guitar player. Paganini preferred to give guitar performances in intimate settings. His rapturous style must have been spellbinding. According to contemporary accounts, Paganini performed like a possessed madman. He was among the first rock musicians, with his flamboyant and reckless lifestyle. He was known to exist between bouts of gambling, drinking, and fiery performances. Paganini wasn't the only major composer to compose for the guitar and perform his guitar compositions. Even Vivaldi wrote compositions for the guitar.

Then there is the litany of other players. I'll mention a few.

Ferdinando Carulli (1770-1841) was regarded as the leading Italian guitarist of his day. Though from Naples, he lived and settled in Paris and enjoyed great success as a composer, performer, and instrument maker. Carulli wrote the first complete classical guitar instruction book and composed over 400 works for the guitar.

Another well-known guitarist from southern Italy was Mauro Giuliani (born in 1781 in Bari, died in Naples in 1829). Giuliani was originally a cellist, but took up the guitar and emigrated to the north, finally settling in Vienna, where he was considered the world's greatest guitarist. He eventually returned to Naples, composing and performing for the royal house of Naples. Giuliani was also a prolific composer, turning out about 200 compositions, many of which remain standards for guitar repertoire. He composed concertos for guitar and orchestra, fantasies and several sonatas for violin and guitar. He also wrote a guitar instruction method.

Why did these composers and musicians leave Naples? T.F. Heck, in "The Role of Italy in the Early History of the Classic Guitar," cites a number of potential reasons: political turmoil caused by Napoleon, too many guitar players in Naples, the emergence of opera, and the lack of Neapolitan music publishers among them. In leaving Naples, its composers exported the Neapolitan sound to the rest of the world.

And all of this history found its way to the United States, specifically to New York City's Little Italy. As I walked the streets of Little Italy with my father when I was a kid, I had no idea that I was strolling in antiquity. When we went to E. Rossi & Company where our family friend Eddie Vecchione worked, I had no idea that the store was once a publishing house that published Neapolitan composers from Italy, Canada, America, and Argentina. I didn't know that Eddie was the uncle of the current owner, Ernie Rossi, or that our family history was bound up with the history of Neapolitan music.

And so now I talk to my father in the form of essays and stories. I've taken a grand tour of the world, having missed the things that were in front of me for most of my childhood. But there's still time for me to do the excavation. And in this process, my father's voice emerges. I hear him talking to me even now as I write this.

Philosophy Major

If taking LSD was good preparation for becoming a philosophy major, I was on track. At eighteen, I was building my career.

"If you take all three hits now, I'll give you the third one for free," said Tom Turkey, the long-haired freak drug dealer. Guys who sold acid in those days would give you powerhouse doses just for kicks. I knew that these two hits wouldn't be ordinary.

My friend Ivan had taken LSD many times before; he would take all of the acid you handed him.

About an hour later, listening to Lothar and the Hand People, I watched the ceiling in Ivan's bedroom melt in slow motion. "Lothar" was like the soundtrack to a horror film. Ivan insisted on listening to deranged music while tripping on acid.

I walked out of the bedroom into his mother's living room. The room looked like the throne of Moses; the golden-paisley decorated couches shone like they belonged in heaven. The lush carpeting ebbed in slow motion like the Red Sea.

Ivan followed me into the living room. He pulled down his chess set from a shelf. He looked like a maniac demon.

I looked down at the chessboard. The chess squares moved around. If I put a piece down, the square changed from black to white, sometimes shading in between. The golden colors of the couch and the brown squares of the chessboard were blinking in unison like Christmas lights.

Running into the kitchen, Ivan returned to the living room table with a butcher's knife and an orange. As he sat down at the table, Ivan pointed the knife at me, then began slicing the orange.

I should have gone home at that moment.

I looked back at him serenely. If he wanted to kill me, someone or something would surely save me. I felt invincible. This is what drugs do to you.

I smiled.

Ivan smiled back.

After cutting the orange open, he began making motions with the knife, pointing at my finger.

I held my hand out to challenge him, as if to say, *Here, cut my finger off if you have the guts*.

We looked into the heaven of our eyeballs.

Suddenly, he slammed the knife down on my finger. Blood spurted out; a purplish red blob splotched the corner of his glasses.

A rush of pain flushed though my body as if someone had dropped an entire building on my finger. The fucking idiot nearly cut my finger off.

#

When I went to New York University two years later, I lived at home and commuted to the Village.

At twenty years old, studying Kierkegaard and reading Hemingway, I had to come home to my father asking me how many pork chops I wanted and listen to his lectures on Jimmy Roselli.

"He sings in the real Neapolitan dialect," my father would repeat endlessly. How many times do you need to tell me this? I thought.

The day I told my mother and father I had just declared myself a philosophy major, they looked shocked.

"What is this philosophy?" my father asked one night at dinner, making it sound like a sinister political orientation. He wasn't ignorant, but he didn't go to college. He hadn't read a philosophy book in his life.

My mother stared at me, watching me hold my fork.

When I had talked about my decision to declare a philosophy major with Ivan a few weeks before, I was triumphant. Ivan of course supported me, in fact, encouraged me. He'd also tried to cut my finger off a few years earlier.

As he choked on the joint he passed me, he said that it was the smart thing to do.

"Dude man, Harrison Ford was a philosophy major. Alex Trebek, too. Besides, dude," he said, tossing back his long mane of unwashed dirty blonde hair, "like, you're into it, man. You've got to groove with what's happening, man. Dude man, like, wherever you are, there you are, you know what I mean? You've got to live out your trip. That's like totally philosophical."

He paused, releasing a plume of pot smoke. "I've decided to go to forestry school, dude. I want to be a forest ranger. Get the fuck out of the city, away from the steel and machines, away from this fucking decay and corruption."

He passed me the joint.

"In this life maybe I'll be a ranger. In another life, man, maybe I'll be like a tree or a bird or a fucking rabbit. Or like, maybe I'll be an alien from another galaxy, man. The thing is you have to find your path, like Don Juan says, man. Your path is philosophy. You can like totally be a philosopher. Go around the world solving problems, getting cats out of their Babylon mind, man."

Now his eyes widened.

"Look man, you can become like a resident philosopher to the Rainbow People. You could travel around man, live in nature, like be totally naked all the time and get high."

I handed him back the joint thinking, *Yeah, I wouldn't mind being a traveling, naked philosopher, smoking weed and meeting pretty hippie girls.* But I also knew it sounded like bullshit.

As I sat at dinner with my parents, I realized that since they were not stoned on weed, my arguments needed to be a little stronger. I wished I could get high with them and discuss my future.

Finally, my mother asked, "What do you study in philosophy?"

"Well, you know, like, you study, like what's the nature of good and bad, what is real —"

She cut me off with a sharp stare, her brown eyes growing smaller and more suspicious by the second. They were blasting out sulfur and fire. Little Sicilian nuclear beetles. Fuming.

She stopped eating. Elbow on the table, holding her fork in midair, she said, "Do you mean to tell me you are working your ass off to pay for a private university education so you can learn about reality? Look around you. Look at this," she shouted, pointing to our project apartment.

She should know. My mother was the rock upon which we all stood. Her face was dark like the earth itself. She trusted things like the soil, water, and the sound of wind. This business of philosophy was bullshit. It didn't put food on the table, or pay the rent.

"Why don't you do something useful like your brother? Business. Medicine. Do something practical."

"It's what I want to do. Harrison Ford was a philosophy major," I said.

My comment was met with a fierce silence.

Then my father shook his head. "We want what's best for you. Neither of us went to college; we didn't have the opportunity. But we know how important it is. It's really not a joking matter."

"Look, I have to study something that can sustain my interest for the next few years."

"The accountant at my job studied accounting in college and then took night classes in subjects he was interested in," said my mother, looking at me like she wanted to bounce my head off the table.

Trying to find a way out of this my father asked, "What can you do with a philosophy major?"

Sitting up straight, I prepared to take on his question. Here was my opportunity to set the record straight. "You can do anything with philosophy."

"Which means it prepares you for nothing in particular," said my father.

"Not really. You learn how to write well, how to think and communicate clearly," I said, realizing how I wasn't demonstrating this so-called skill. I lamely tried to defend myself. I wished I could employ the Socratic method on them to make my point, cornering them with clever questions until I forced them to agree with me.

In a desperate grasp for something hopeful to say, I repeated what my Philosophy of Mind professor had said earlier in the semester.

"Philosophy majors frequently go into law school. They handed out an article in class last week saying that philosophy majors score highest on the LSAT test."

My mother relaxed her shoulders, loosened the granite look on her face. "So you want to be a lawyer?" she asked in her Lower East Side accent.

For a moment I was victorious. They were both basking in my glorious future. Out of the projects, law degree in hand. Backyard. Plush carpet, not like the tattered mat in our living room.

I let the moment last.

"Well, ah, not exactly," I said.

They looked at each other, then back at me.

"Well, you know, I wouldn't want to represent the law in this country. We live in a diseased society. A society that condones slavery, empire building, environmental destruction, and is indifferent to the life of the soul." At that moment, I hated myself for sounding like Ivan.

"Is this what you study in philosophy?" my father asked, as if I'd been attending satanic rituals, eating raw animal flesh, and drinking animal blood from a chalice.

"Not exactly. This is just stuff on my mind."

"You've got to grow up, kid. You've got to do something with your life. Believe me; I know how important making money is. I know. You don't want to live like we have. That's what I'm trying to tell you, goddammit."

"You're right. I don't want to live like we have." We lived in the projects. My father's gambling chained to all of our necks.

"Don't be a smartass. We're trying to help you. Someday you'll understand."

I wanted to say, *Why did you encourage me to go to school in the first place?* But I just said, "I know, Dad, I know," rolling my eyes, hating them for not understanding the predicament they put me in.

The Ring

Walking into my mother and father's bedroom, I go straight to her chest of drawers. She keeps her jewelry in a little compartment next to her undergarments. The ring is there, just like I expected it to be. I pick up the ring and look at it. It's made of white gold and studded with diamonds. Up until then I had just been stealing little things: necklaces, earrings, and things that didn't get noticed. A little bit at a time. Then I'd go down to the husband and wife jewelers on Steinway Street and sell them for what I could get. They'd weigh the gold and give me money, maybe twenty or thirty dollars. Knowing it was stolen, and that I was a dumb kid, they gave me less than market value.

I hear the apartment door opening, so I grab the ring and shove it into my pants pocket. Taking big steps, I rush out to the living room, out of breath.

My father drops his keys on the table, looking at me suspiciously.

"Home from school already?" he asks.

"Yeah, we got out early," I say.

"Are you doing laps in the house?" he asks.

"Push-ups," I say quickly, catching my breath.

"Oh, okay. Do you want to go for a slice of pizza?" he asks.

"No." I'm brimming with guilt right now; I don't want to be around my father. The ring is burning a hole in my pocket. I'm imagining the guitar I could buy with this ring. It's got to be worth many hundreds of dollars. I could buy a white Fender Stratocaster like the one Jimi Hendrix plays. I'll probably have enough left over to play video games at the smoke shop. For a few weeks, I'm going to live it up.

And I'll get away with it. Right now, my mother is furious at my father. Night after night, she yells at him at the dining room table.

"How can you just sit there?" she asks.

He doesn't say anything.

She takes another sip of red wine. Her words begin to slur.

"Get another job. You – have – to – do – something." She shouts the words one at a time, as if not speaking in sentences.

He doesn't look up. He keeps looking down at the crossword puzzle on the table, smoking his cigarette, tapping ashes in the ashtray. Unlike my mother, my father doesn't drink. Gambling has destroyed him enough. He remains sober, all too aware of the pain he's caused his wife, his children.

"We don't have anything. You keep lying, you keep gambling and we don't have anything. We can't pay the rent this month. We – can't – pay – the – rent."

My mother's not going to think I stole her ring; she's going to think my father did. He's the one who needs the money.

I leave the apartment and go up to the sixth floor where my best friend Lan lives.

"I got the ring," I say.

"You took the ring?" he asks, wincing. We'd talked about it, but he can't believe that I would do something so bold, so evil. Lan is like a brother to me. Being half Puerto Rican and half black, he's slightly darker than I am.

"Yes," I say, smiling but worried. This was my mother's favorite ring.

"What are you going to do?" he asks.

"I'm going to sell it at the jewelry store," I say. "Let's go now. I can't keep this thing in my pocket."

We walk to the jewelry store on Steinway Street. He can't get over how gutsy this move is.

We get to the store. The owner is reading a newspaper.

"What do you have today?" he asks. He puts the newspaper down and reaches for his magnifying glass.

I hand him the ring.

He looks at the ring and then looks at me. He applies a liquid to the ring to determine the amount of gold alloy.

He calls his wife over.

I can tell he's trying to hide his excitement. His wife looks closely at the ring, then looks at me. I can see she's excited too. This is an antique ring, with delicate designs and settings. The diamonds are subtle, but they shimmer.

"How much do you want?" he asks.

"How much do you think it's worth?" I ask.

"I don't know, maybe three hundred," he says, waving his hand, like he's not that interested.

"Three hundred and fifty?"

He looks at his wife; she bites her lip, nodding in agreement.

"So three hundred and fifty?" he says.

"Yes," I say, my voice trailing away, now realizing I could have gotten more. But three hundred and fifty should be enough to buy a guitar.

His wife goes to the register to get the money and hands it to her husband.

He counts out six fifties, two twenties, and one ten in my hand.

"Three hundred and fifty."

I look down at the money.

"So, okay?" the man says.

I'm hesitant to walk away from the deal.

"Okay?" he repeats. He can't believe his luck.

I fold the money up and put it in my pocket. The man then hands the ring to his wife. It's a gift from him to her and for a great price.

#

"I can't find my ring," my mother says, storming out of the room. She looks at my father.

"What?"

"Have you seen my ring?"

"Me?" he says.

"Yes, you. I'm talking to you," she shouts at my dad. I knew it would go this way.

"Did you see the ring?" she now points at me and asks.

"Uh, no," I say, shocked.

My mother is rabid. She tries to light a cigarette but can't because her nerves are shaken. She throws the matches across the table.

"Maybe it was the maintenance man," my father says. He lights a cigarette too.

My brother Frank and my sisters, Camille and Lynn, are now in the living room. It's a witch hunt. My father is the one with blood on his hands. My hands are alabaster white.

"Frank, if you did this," my mother says, now crying, "I'll never talk to you again, you fucking bastard. You know how much that ring meant to me."

"I would never do that to you," he says, nervously smoking. He can't help but be guilty. He's always guilty. He's the one who lies, borrows, and steals. He's the one who could steal the ring, who would steal the ring to get more money to gamble or to pay off an urgent debt. Except he would have gotten eight hundred to a thousand for the ring. With that thousand dollars he could have placed a few bets at the horse track, he could have been a sport for a few days, taking us out to a Chinese restaurant, buying comics for me and my brother. That's what he loved most about money. He loved to spend money on other people, show them that he could.

But not me. I'm greedy. I think about how smart I am. I've outsmarted them all. Only twelve years old and I've tricked them all. While I ran away with the golden egg, my father is nailed to the cross. He deserves to be the one nailed to the cross. He's the one who fucked up, not me.

As my mother rants, I'm thinking about the guitar I'm going to buy. It's going to be beautiful, just like the guitar Hendrix played at Woodstock. Beaming in brilliant white, with a whammy bar. When I play it, I'll sound just like Hendrix, roaring, on fire, thrusting my body back and forth, as I pull the strings, the notes shooting out like flaming bullets.

Killing Time

Bruno had Jimmy Roselli smack dead in his scope. All he had to do was pull the trigger and it was all over. Then, Roselli hit a high note that stunned Bruno. Bruno held the trigger, then eased it back into a rest position. This Roselli guy could really fucking sing.

Roselli finished the song then took a bow to the audience. The old men and women gave him a resounding round of applause. The girls squirmed in their seats, legs crossing and uncrossing. The boys tried desperately to hide their tears.

It's really a shame, thought Bruno as he again raised the .38 to his squinting eye. This guy is terrific.

As he tried to place Roselli's head in the crosshairs of the scope, the orchestra began the familiar opening music of "Malafemmena." Roselli walked back and forth on the stage.

He pulled the hammer back to unload the bullet.

Now Bruno recalled his mother sitting on the couch doing needlework from morning until night. She sat on the couch wearing a *malocchio* pendant and a clove of garlic. She touched the *malocchio*, then the garlic, made the sign of the cross, then tapped each kid on the head. No witch would hurt her or her family.

Bruno lowered the gun. Too many memories rushing into his mind. He gently eased the hammer back, his thumb carefully gripping it until it settled back down into place.

"Malafemmena" means bad woman. It's a song about a man whose heart is broken – kind of like a Neapolitan "Lovesick Blues." Boy meets girl, falls in love – she loves another, maybe a few – boy gets a heartache. Bruno reminisced about pretty Angela Modina, a girl he dated. Angela had a face like white porcelain, perfect pink lips and curves like a tulip. He loved that she smelled like a flower. But she didn't love him. He took her to the Copa, front row seats, to see Bobby Darin, Tony Bennett, bought her expensive jewelry. In his heart, though, he knew why she didn't love him. He had a big head, like a horse, enormous yellow teeth, some bunched together and some missing. His hands were swollen and coarse from all the shoveling he did. She knew what he did, knew he wasn't in contracting like he claimed.

"We're just not right for each other," said Angela one night at the Copa. She gently let go of his hand, got up and walked out of his life forever.

Tears now running down his pudgy, acned cheeks, Bruno could hardly see Roselli, his eyes too filled with water. He stuffed the gun in his belt and reached for the handkerchief in the inner pocket of his suit jacket. They said that Roselli made even the wise guys weep. He thought that was a joke – an exaggeration. Here he was, hired to gun Roselli down in cold blood – like he'd done to others many times before. He'd knocked off good ones, bad ones – never a pause, or a hitch. He even popped a priest who was on the take. But he couldn't kill this so-called singer.

#

Later, Bruno sat in Sam Giancarlo's office, trying to explain.

"You realize I could just shoot you right now," shouted Sam. "The prick makes me look ridiculous, telling Tony the Tuna he ain't gonna give no vig for his shows," he said, scolding Bruno, snapping his pointed index finger and thumb like a revolver. "Who the fuck does he think he is? Sinatra, Darin, Bennett and the others make their payments."

Bruno opened his mouth.

Sam interrupted, continuing.

"What do I have to do? Kill the shithead myself?" He pursed his lips, shrugged his shoulders. His face was red as a radish. "What's your excuse?"

Bruno couldn't get a word in.

"You don't have a fucking excuse."

"But …"

"Let me tell you something, you made him look legitimate. The guy's a loser. I've ruined his career, destroyed his big-label contracts. The guy sells albums out of the back of his car in Little Italy," said Sam, practically running out of breath, exasperated. "He's like a roach I can't stomp out. This is why I wanted you to shoot him in front of all of his goddamn adoring fans. One in the head, so they have nightmares every time they hear his fucking music."

Sam took a pill for indigestion with a glass of water. His eyes streaked with bulging capillaries, red and watery.

"You won't have another shot after this time. Understand?" shouted Sam, raising his eyebrows. "Here's what you gotta do," he continued, holding his groin as he spoke.

"Reach down, grab your balls and make sure they are there, then pull the fucking trigger." He paused. "Eh?" he asked, waiting for a response, preferably one without words.

Bruno grunted from his belly.

Sitting in his study that night, Sam Giancarlo looked through his family book of pastry recipes. It was the only thing that relaxed him nowadays. That and listening to Jerry Vale. Jerry Vale soothed him like rain water, set his soul at rest.

As he thumbed through the handwritten pages of recipes, he heard Jerry Vale's version of "Mama." He recalled sitting on his mother's lap, as a boy, noticing how big and strong her hands were.

He heard a knock at the door.

His mother, Carmella, walked in and sat down on the couch across from him. She took out her knitting needles and embroidery.

"So, you're nervous?" she asked.

"I'm not nervous."

"Whenever you read my book of pastry recipes I know you're nervous," she said looking down at her embroidery. The design depicted a horse and carriage, in Christmas red and green. There were embroideries around the horse, the result of many restless nights.

"This is my favorite," said Sam, pointing to one of the pastry recipes. "*Belli e Brutti*." He recalled the buttery aroma that filled the house when his mother baked them.

"That recipe came from a long line of mothers," she said, her big hands working the needles expertly. Her hands were bony, but like steel. The veins bulged over her knuckles. You could tell that her hands had never stopped working, never stopped making things.

"I know about the Roselli thing," she said.

Sam looked up from the book, then at her.

She continued needling, not meeting his eyes.

From the record player, Jerry Vale, meanwhile, broke into the chorus of "Mama."

"I don't like this business," she said.

Still amazed, he didn't say anything.

"It's not good, I tell you, and I don't like it. This Roselli is the best we have. He's got the heart of a bear. And the balls of a bull. Out of all of them, he's the only one who stands alone and says no to you."

"He's a troublemaker, mama. We can't let it stand," he replied, plopping an Alka-Seltzer in a glass of water.

"Listen – don't you think I know? I was with your father for forty years. When you were still in diapers, I'd already seen it all. I've seen them come and go," she said, now looking at her son's face, pausing from her needlework. "This one is different. He has the voice of an angel. I know he's a ball breaker. But you've made him suffer. He's a nobody and can't hardly get no job in this city. He sells his music from a cart, like a *shtoonda* ice-cream man."

"What's done is done."

"What do you mean?" she asked, raising her voice, her dark eyes on fire.

"I mean we've sent out for another job."

"Mama" rang out now, Jerry Vale's voice loudly declaring the love of mother and son, as if from the top of a mountain.

"Is this what you want?" she said, pointing to the speakers. "This half-man. He doesn't even sing in real Neapolitan. Nat King Cole sings better Neapolitan than he does." She looked back down, resuming the knitting. The long green needles working furiously in her hands. "Your father loved Roselli. He hated this Jerry Vale."

"I know, mama," he replied like a scolded son. "But the job is on its way."

His mother stormed out of the study, making the *malocchio* sign with her pinky, index and thumb extended.

Sam noticed the green knitting needles left on the couch. His mother had many sets of green needles; it was her favorite color.

#

Strapping his shoulder holster to his body, Bruno prepared to leave, while listening to Jerry Vale's "O Sole Mio."

He took a shot of whiskey and looked in the mirror, saying Hail Marys in Italian.

As he recited the Hail Mary, Bruno felt a sudden bolt of pain in his left temple. In the mirror he saw a long green needle sticking out of his head. For a split second he was totally confused, then his mind vacated his body. As the blood trickled down his head, his eyes closed. A second later, he died.

#

The next morning Sam Giancarlo entered the kitchen for breakfast. On the table sat a plate of *Belli e Brutti*, freshly cooked.

He slid into a chair and put one of the cookies in his mouth.

His mother walked into the kitchen.

"How about we listen to Roselli's *Malafemmena*?" she asked.

Sam stood still not sure what to say or do. Roselli would be dead by now; playing his music would be in bad taste.

"I want to listen to it now. I'm going to the Copa tonight. Roselli's performing," she said.

Has the old lady lost her marbles, Sam wondered?

"But mom, didn't we —" he started to say.

"He'll be there tonight," she said, working the green needles. "Trust me. He's the hardest working one of them all. And the best."

He stared at her. For a moment, he was angry. But only for a moment. Then a warm glow poured over his face. Mama mia! This crazy lady. This beautiful crazy lady.

"Have your Belli e Brutti," she said. "I made them just for you, figlio mio."

Ringing Bells

My father parked across from the Off Track Betting entrance. As we crossed the street, he put his hand on my shoulder. His touch was welcome, but unexpected.

My father, at six feet one, stood like a mountain. Even his distended belly seemed like a bulging cliff. On Saturday mornings, I used to climb into his bed and rest my head on his stomach, making fun of how big it was.

"Stop, I'm trying to sleep," he'd say, but he wouldn't shove me off.

Now at the OTB, approaching a betting window, my father pulled out a wad of twenty-dollar bills from his pocket.

I watched him plunk them down one by one, then looked up at him. It was the most money I had ever seen in one pile.

"Why are you betting this money?"

Suddenly, he became distant.

"It's not worth anything to me as it is." He didn't look me in the face. He took a drag on his cigarette and looked out into the street.

There must be about three hundred dollars there, I guessed. Even at twelve years old, I knew the recklessness of my father putting that money down.

"When you need five thousand dollars, three hundred dollars ain't nothing," said my father flatly.

Even if three hundred dollars wasn't five thousand dollars, it was still three hundred dollars more than nothing. My family needed the money.

Leaving the betting windows, burrowing through a cloud of thick, stale smoke, we walked toward the exit. My father clutched the tickets in his hand.

As we stepped outside of the OTB, he greeted his friend, Augie. I'd seen Augie before.

My father smiled reaching out to shake Augie's hand.

"Is this little Mickey?" asked Augie, looking at me. "He gets bigger every time I see him."

Augie's eyes were red. He looked like he hadn't shaved for weeks; the stubble on his face was pointy and reddish, slightly graying on the fringes. Chest hairs poked out of his buttoned yellowed shirt. Augie drank coffee and smoked constantly, sometimes pulling an inch at a time off the cigarette with each drag. His breath smelled like the sour smoke of a public toilet.

I didn't really listen as my dad and Augie talked, though I heard fragments of their conversation. I was too absorbed by Augie's face to hear anything. I noticed how his scabby lips curled, and how his rusted teeth looked like a city of broken buildings.

Then the race began.

Augie and my father motioned for me to follow them back into the OTB. As we hurried into the entrance, I saw an old woman in a blue dress with yellow flowers filling out a betting form. She held a cigarette nervously, leaving red lipstick rings on the filter. As I looked around, I noticed that there were many different kinds of people in this place. Short, old wrinkled-faced men. Tall, skinny sunken-faced women. Even young people. No one looked joyful.

We stared up at the little OTB television screen. My father crossed his arms, looking broad and large, like a monument. He held a cigarette in his left hand and clutched his tickets with his right hand, making a fist. He squeezed the tickets as though he was trying to extract blood from them.

I knew that my father bet on the horse with the red banner. Different-colored banners over the horses' backs helped identify them as they raced around the track. They had names, of course, but I paid attention to the colors.

I had learned a trick from my father. If I wanted a horse to win, I'd steady my eyes on it, repeating win, win, win to myself. In this case, I wanted the horse with the red banner, my dad's horse, to win. After focusing on the winning horse, I'd hex the horse I didn't want to win, chanting jinx, jinx, jinx over and over again in my head. I had used the trick last week watching the Knicks game, putting a spell on the Lakers. The Knicks went ahead of the Lakers in the last two minutes and hung on to win.

Then the race started.

Augie's horse, the one with the yellow banner, left the gate with a jump and was a few necks ahead in seconds. Augie excitedly thrust the rolled-up betting form in the air, exposing the faded tattoo of an anchor on the sagging fat of his right arm. On his left arm was a barely visible image of Christ's head with the thorny crown jammed into his scalp. Christ looked upward with saddened eyes.

I assumed my father had chosen me to join him at the OTB, or come with him to bars, because he knew I wouldn't say anything, ever. Maybe he thought that my older brother Renato might tell my mother. More than once, my father took me to the bar on Crescent Street in Astoria. I played the stand-up bowling machine while my father went into the private room behind the bar. I knew the bar was run by mobsters.

Watching the television screen, Augie's horse was winning, with my father's in third place. A horse wearing a green banner was second.

It was now the third and last lap.

"Go, you son-of-a-bitch," shouted Augie. He cupped his hands around his mouth as he whispered to my father, "There's no way I can lose here."

My father stood stoic, only twitching his eyes, as the smoke from his cigarette curled up and licked his flittering eyelids.

I now vigorously jinxed the horse with the yellow banner, hurling a plague in its direction, praying furiously that the jockey would fall off or the horse would break a leg, or die.

Augie's horse seemed to fall back slowly, overtaken by my dad's horse. Then suddenly the horse with the green banner was neck and neck with my dad's horse.

My jinx had sent Augie's horse into fifth place; the horse was definitely out of the race. Augie slapped his rolled-up betting form into his hand and said "Jesus goddamned Christ."

The horses were about fifty yards from the finish line. They were moving fast, kicking up mud, their riders sitting high up on the saddle.

I could tell my father was also using the jinx by his blinking eyes. My father's horse would inch ahead any second now. I sent hexes from my eyes to the horse with the green banner. Jinx on you green horse, jinx you to hell you son-of-a-bitch. Fall down, die.

I looked at my dad's horse, win, this is all of the money my father has, win, win, win.

My father looked at me and winked. I was busy managing all of the evil and good gremlins at play.

Now everyone leaned toward the television screen.

The horse wearing the green banner jumped a neck ahead. He crossed the finish line first. How did that happen? The crowd seemed to recoil.

Just like that, the race was over. The winning jockey stood up on his horse pushing his fists in the air victoriously.

My father fluttered his lips, blowing air out, like a punctured balloon. I watched his right hand loosen, his fingers uncoiling their grip. The losing tickets, mangled and wet from the sweat on his hand, fell to the already cluttered floor. I could see disappointment in my father's face, no matter how much he tried to hold it in. I hated when I saw that look.

All I could think about was that pile of twenty-dollar bills stacked up like a mountain of money, more than I'd ever seen.

And now it was all gone.

The Angry Howl

"You don't know nothing about music," my father says, driving in his Dodge Dart, making a left turn under the El. At sixteen, I know everything about music.

It's raining. Driving to Pete the butcher's, who has a shop on 31st Street under the elevated train station, I can't look away from the dull concrete streets. Hookers and crackheads walk the streets at night. Here, in the midst of the littered pavement, with blood and cum filling the sidewalk crevices, Pete sells his specialty Italian sausages, prosciuttos and salamis. On Easter, you see the goats hanging on meat hooks, the wool sheared from their bodies.

Instead of arguing, I roll my eyes.

My father slides the eight-track into the tape chamber. "Ted Fiorito was one of the great bandleaders of all time," he says, with a boastful smirk, making his nose protrude more than it already does. But does he know that Fiorito wrote "Toot Toot Tootsie?" Or that Muzzy Marcellino and Candy Candido were members of the Fiorito Orchestra? Whether or not he knew them, he knew this music. He knew it in his bones.

"That's why I play this music for you," my dad says, now making the music louder. We drive with the music filling the car. We don't speak until he pulls the car to the curb.

"The best musicians and singers are Italian," says my father, parking near Pete's butcher shop. "But you don't know that," he says. I don't answer.

Pete's smells of cheeses, olives and salamis. A sweet smell. Big and short salamis hang from the ceiling. There are barrels with olives and cheeses on the counter.

My father pays for the salamis and sausages and hands me the bags. We walk back to the car.

"The Italians, they're just wops to you, right?" he asks, stopping near the car. He opens the door on his side.

"You've never been called a wop, I bet," he says. "They called me wop when I was a kid," he says. "The Irish, mostly, but not only. But I didn't give a shit. They were white bread and butter. What the hell did they know? They didn't have Caruso, they didn't have Sinatra. What'd they have? Crosby?"

He then puts the key in the car, sits down, reaches over and opens my door.

I get back into the car. He starts the car and immediately turns the radio dial to make it louder. It's Sinatra. His voice fills the car.

"There is no one like Sinatra," he says. The words, like heat, rise up my neck, sink into the base of my skull. The feeling is animal, like the ancient reptile in me is woken. "Crosby is a cold fish compared to this," he says. "You know why the Italians are the great singers?" he asked.

"I don't know."

"Because we're tough. When you dig ditches, when you take shit from people who think they're better, when you can't speak their language, it makes you angry. When you're angry, you sing like you mean it," he says.

Separation

"Why did we separate?" My son Theo asks. He's seven years old.

"We're not separated now, right? I'm with you tonight," I say. "Today is Monday and I will see you Wednesday, and Friday too."

We're drawing; we always talk when we draw. I can never get him to talk if I just ask him questions directly. I bought us each a drawing pad. I want him to do his own drawings. He often looks at my drawing and wants to draw in my book. But then I start drawing on his pad. If he likes what I've done, he'll take over and make his own drawing. Beginning is hard.

"Where's your father?" he asks.

"My father died," I tell him.

"Where'd he go?"

"I don't know."

"What was your dad like?" He's coloring a picture now. It's a multi-colored house – with a winding pathway in the back that leads to a patch of hills. There's a sign on the house that says "Teddy and Papa's Candyhouse."

"He was tall – he had a deep voice."

"Did he look like you?"

"Not really. I look more like Grandma." I inherited the Sicilian genes; I'm short and squat, like I was born to hammer stone. My father – his grandfather – was a tall Neapolitan with a proud Neapolitan nose.

"What did he do?"

"He worked in computers like me."

"How old was he when he died?"

"Sixty-two."

"How old are you?"

"Thirty-five," I say.

"How old were you when he died?"

"I was about twenty-six." His eyes look off to the side; he's calculating how much time I have left.

"Did your dad draw?"

"Yes he did. I'll show you the drawings; I can bring them from grandma's house."

"Did you draw with him?"

"No – not like we do."

"Why?"

"I don't know."

My father would draw superheroes for me and my brother. He'd start before we went to bed; I remember the smell of the marker ink. I tell my son that my father could draw from comic books, or from pictures in the newspaper.

"Can you draw like that?"

"No. I draw less realistically."

"Why don't you draw like your dad?"

"I've really never tried. I like the way I draw."

I ask him, "Do you like when we draw together?"

"Yes."

"Why?"

"It's fun. I like how you draw and we get to tell jokes to each other. I want to draw as well as you someday."

I tell him that there are no mistakes when you draw; it's all for play.

"Do you have fun?" he asks, not looking up from his drawing. He's concentrating on making a circle.

"Yes," I tell him. "I love drawing with you." We're still reeling from the separation and pending divorce. I am shaken from everything. Being with him now is paradise.

Weeks later, I get my father's drawing pads from my mother's house. They were up in a closet, packed in a plastic storage bag. I haven't seen them in years. There are caricatures of famous singers and musicians: Dean Martin, Frank Sinatra, Tony Bennett, and Louis Prima. My son is stunned.

"Your dad did these?"

"Yes."

"He didn't do this for a living?"

"No – he did these for fun."

"We should draw like this for fun, too."

I try to copy the picture of Sinatra. The detailed lines of the blue hat he's wearing are very delicate and precise. What looks like a few easy brush strokes proves to be deceptively difficult. The green color of his tie compliments the sparkling blue of his eyes. These are remarkable drawings.

"Why didn't your father draw for a living?"

"I don't know – he probably didn't know he could. He worked in computers. He never studied drawing."

"Would you work in drawing if you could draw like this?"

"Yes." I think of all of the things I love to do: write, play music, draw. Yet, I too work in computers.

"Are you like your dad?"

"Yes and no," I say.

"How so?"

"Hard to explain."

"Did you draw and play sports with your dad like we do?"

"No - but we did things."

"Like what?"

"Listened to music, watched movies together – watched football."

"So you did stuff with him like we do."

"Yes. I guess you're right."

"Were you ever separated from your dad?"

"Only briefly; he left for a few weeks."

"But you got back together?"

"Yes we did."

"You were lucky then."

"You're lucky too."

"Yes, but we separated."

"We're together now."

"But it's different."

"Yes, I guess you're right. It's different."

The Patron Saint of Second Avenue

My father talked to me about his uncle, Virgilio Vignola, for as long as I could remember. But it was as if Virgilio was either dead or lived on the other side of the world. He was neither. While we lived in Queens, just across from the Fifty-Ninth Street Bridge, Virgilio lived in a five-story walk-up apartment building in Manhattan on Second Avenue at Twelfth Street.

"Why don't you visit him?" I asked my father.

"I haven't seen him in twenty years, since my father died."

"You can visit him now, right?"

"He's a private person," said my father. "He doesn't want to be in touch."

"Does he have a phone number?"

"I don't think he has a phone, or at least he doesn't give out his number."

My father told me that the last time he had visited Virgilio was with my mother and his sister, Anne. In 1955.

"We had just gotten married. At that time, Virgilio still entertained guests, though he never came to family events and never to anyone's house."

"Where did he live then?" I asked.

"In a tenement apartment on Second Avenue, before they tore them all down." He paused. "He was crazy, Virgilio."

"What do you mean?"

"Let me tell you. When we went to his house, he greets us at the door in a red velvet smoking jacket." Now my father started to laugh a little.

"He walks us from the door to his living room, puffing a long cigarette in a fancy cigarette holder. You have to understand, the entire apartment is decorated like the inside of a navy ship."

I waited for him to continue.

"He was in the Navy during World War II. And he was this incredible genius. He built portal windows like you'd see in a navy ship and mounted them on the walls. He replaced the bathroom door with naval ship compartment doors. And he hung an anchor on the wall. The living room looked like the helm of a ship, with a steering wheel built into the floor."

"So what happened then?"

"He walks us into his apartment and introduces us to Haiku, who he refers to as his manservant."

"How could he afford a manservant?"

"He was probably his boyfriend," said my father. "At that time, people didn't always talk so openly about those things."

"So he was gay?"

"Yes, he was gay," replied my father, nodding his head. "Then, he sits us down in the living room and offers to play the piano for us. On the piano is a silver candelabra. The house is dimly lit, the candles flickering shadows on the walls. He starts playing this beautiful classical piece. I don't know what it was. I have to admit, it's pretty amazing. But my sister, Anne, being the person she is, asks him if he could play something ragtime. Virgilio doesn't appreciate the comment. He rolls his eyes a bit then starts playing a ragtime piece. He quickly gets bored and then he resumes playing classical."

"Why do you think he was annoyed at being asked to play a ragtime piece?"

"Virgilio wanted to do what he wanted to do. And people always wanted him to be what they wanted him to be. The guy could do anything. He worked for the police as a police sketcher. He played several instruments. He even performed some medical procedures."

"Where did he learn how to do these things?"

"I have no idea. He must have read books in the library. But he also had enormous ability. His mother thought he was a genius," my father said.

"One time, his mother asked him to lance a mole off of her face; she had complete confidence in her son. He said he could do it. The family was worried that he'd make her bleed to death or maybe give her an infection. He'd never done anything like this before. But no, he performs the procedure and it's perfect. The mole came off without a hitch."

"That's amazing!"

"Wait, it gets crazier," said my father. "After the mole procedure, he started calling himself a doctor. Dr. Vignola. His father, who had worked on the railroads, had bad feet. He started to complain about his toe. Virgilio offered to cut his toe off. He said that the toe was corrupted and would only get infected or worse over time. Now, unlike his mother, Virgilio's father was always a little afraid of Virgilio. For years, his father used to say that he was afraid to sleep at night, so he slept with the lights on."

"Did he ever perform the toe procedure?" I asked.

"No, by the time Virgilio's father died, his toe curled up into his foot, like a turtle's head escaping into its shell. He even started sleeping with shoes on, too. In fact, he slept with shoes on both feet, so Virgilio wouldn't cut the toe off of either foot." My father laughed a little. "I think he drove the old man a little crazy."

"That's hysterical," I said. "But why was Virgilio so private," I asked. It sounded like he withdrew from his family over time.

"Well," my father started, "first of all, being gay, he was concerned that his family would judge him, which they did. He didn't have kids. He wasn't interested in anyone else's kids. *Why was he so selfish*, they'd say. *Why doesn't he come to weddings, funerals, and on the holidays?* He didn't really like being treated as odd, though he didn't really do anything to change anyone's opinion of him. He was different. He was extraordinary. He had great things on his mind. But he was surrounded by ordinary people."

"Do you think he would be okay if I visited him now?" I asked.

"You could try," said my father. "He might yell at you and tell you to leave." I shrugged like I wouldn't care if he did. "I think he hangs out at the candy store on Second Avenue and Twelfth Street still," he added.

I finally worked up the courage to go visit Virgilio. I was afraid that I'd be intruding on his world. But I had to meet this man.

My father told me stories about some of the eccentric artist types in his family, but I'd never met any of them. Virgilio was the crown jewel of them all.

I took a bus from Eighty-Eighth Street and Second Avenue, filled with anticipation. It was like we had a Michelangelo or a da Vinci in our family.

I got off the bus at Twelfth Street and ambled over to the candy store.

"Excuse me," I said to the man behind the counter. "Do you know a man named Virgilio?"

"Who?" replied the man, acting like I was wasting his time.

"Virgilio, doesn't he hang out here?"

"I don't know nobody by that name."

"He lives in the building next to the store," I said.

"Like I said, I don't know nobody with that name," barked the man now, as he stacked a pile of newspapers on the counter.

I walked out of the store, my shoulders slumped over. I had thought that meeting Virgilio would help me find a missing piece to the puzzle of my family. Like Virgilio, my father was a very talented self-taught artist. He even once carved a chess piece out of chalk for my sister's school project for which she'd won an award. He had never carved anything before.

My father made caricatures of famous people, like Duke Ellington and Dean Martin, using colored ink pens. He had a very unique sense of developing patterns and using bold colors. He also did pencil sketches. My mother kept his drawings in the closet for years. I've since framed some of them and have digitized most of the colored ink pictures.

The link to all of this was Virgilio; he was the artistic patron saint of our family. He was misunderstood, perhaps ridiculed. For being different, for being gay. For being talented. And because of this, he shunned our family. There was a precious history to the man.

But Virgilio would remain a ghost to me. I'd never meet the man. After my father died, I forgot about Virgilio for a number of years. I never even thought about him, until my mother brought him up, reminding me of the stories. She also said that my father's cousin did genealogical research. Supposedly the name Vignola came from the north of Italy and was associated with artisans. I didn't believe this. Southern Italians want to believe that they had roots in the north. Instead of thinking themselves potato farmers and peasants from the south, they'd invent an imagined aristocratic past. But I didn't believe it.

I never even knew when, if or how Virgilio died. He must have lived out his life the way he wanted to, without judgment. He seemed to vanish from the earth without anyone from our family even knowing.

The last time my father talked about Virgilio he described one of the paintings he made that hung in the hallway.

"What really stood out about the painting was the stunning colors and patterns. The way he placed bold colors next to each other and his imaginative use of design. The way he painted made you look at the world in a different way."

I didn't realize it then, but that's exactly the way I now describe my father's own drawings.

Staying Home

"I dream about you a lot these days," I say to my dad.

"And for some reason I show up in your dreams," he says, laughing.

It doesn't feel like I'm dreaming.

His voice is clear. The wisps of his gray hair are fine and crisp.

I see the individual strands layered on top of each other. I always forget that I'm dreaming until he reminds me. He seems so real.

"I think it's because I'm getting older that I dream more of you. Not to mention that stress makes me crazy," I say.

"You have no idea the stress I had, being in debt and watching my family suffer." His face looks sad and heavy. "A gambler can't help himself," he says.

"I know. I think about it sometimes. I can't believe you were able to take it."

"Your mother was angry and she had a right to be. We were the only white people left in the projects. I ain't never had nothing against black people, but even they didn't want to be there. And if living in the projects wasn't bad enough, we were kicked out when they found out your mother worked. It could have been so much better." Then he looks at me. "I wasn't there for you."

"You were there for me," I say. "We got out of the projects, I went to college. So much of what I've done is because of you." *What have I done?* I wonder as I'm saying this.

"I could have given you more."

"You gave me a lot. You gave me your attention and time. You were always home. In fact, you hardly went out," I say laughing a little. "For a gambler in debt, you were home a lot."

"It's not funny."

"I know, it's not," I say. "You gave me Sinatra. You taught me how to love music. And you showed me how to respect women."

"Do you know how beautiful your mother was when I met her?"

"You told us all of the time. I hear you in my head when I tell my wife she's beautiful."

He pauses at what I've just said.

"You know some men are millionaires and beat their wives," I say.

"You married a good woman," he says. "Not an Italian. But a good woman."

"How do you know?" I ask. He ignores my question.

"I tell Theo about you all of the time. He feels gypped," I say.

"You can't blame me for dying."

"You didn't take care of yourself and you worried yourself sick."

"Are you going to lecture me now? I'm dead already."

"But we wanted more of you. We needed more of you. Mom needed more of you."

He sighs.

"When you were alive, you had two grandchildren. After you died, there were eight more. I have two kids now."

He smiles, shaking his head like he knows this already.

"And Frank became a millionaire. You could have borrowed a lot of money from him," I say.

He looks angrily at me. "I wouldn't have borrowed money from my son."

We look at each other knowing he would have.

"I need you now. I need to talk to you about life decisions. I need your support."

"We're talking now."

"But I'm dreaming."

"I can't do anything about that. Do you think I know what this is all about?"

"You know, when I was a kid I dreamt that I met you when you were a boy. My favorite superhero was Captain America because he was your favorite superhero. In my dream we went to the comic book store together and bought the first Captain America comic book."

"I think I had a dream like that, too," he says. "That's strange."

"I've always remembered that dream. I had to be about eleven," I say.

"We're more similar than you ever wanted to admit."

I don't respond.

"You'll soon be dead longer than I knew you when you were alive," I say.

"It's twenty years now," he says.

"You're more real in my dreams than you were when I was a kid. I can talk to you as a man now."

"Yes, you're a man now."

"There's so much I want to tell you," I say realizing I'm telling him. "Remember that store you used to take me to on Grand Street, the one where Eddie worked? They sell Italian music and Neapolitan coffee pots?"

"E. Rossi & Company," he says without hesitation.

"I go there now and play guitar with the owner's grandson."

"Ernie?" he asks. "I told you that you'd grow up some day and like that music."

"I grew up."

We look at each other silently.

"Will I see you again?"

"I'm not sure," he says.

Small Matters

We got the call at 5 a.m. My father had woken from a coma after forty-eight hours and asked to see his family.

Before he had fallen into the coma, we had brought him home from the hospital.

"Take him home and make him comfortable; he doesn't have long," the doctor said.

We came home and ordered food. For my father, we ordered angel-hair pasta with shrimp. My mother, his wife for nearly forty years, tried to help him sit up and eat, but he could barely lift the fork to his mouth. Eating was more of a gesture than a reality.

In three months, he turned bone white as the cancer tore through him. The doctors were right, despite my mother's condemnation of medicine and all science.

"I don't trust those damned doctors," she said, her dark Sicilian eyes swelling behind her thick reading glasses. After two thousand years of being run over by invading foreigners, Sicilians had faith only in family.

"He didn't get this from smoking, you know," she said to me.

"He has pancreas cancer," she continued, raising her voice, as she lit a cigarette. "You don't get pancreas cancer from smoking."

We'd had this discussion plenty of times, so I didn't say anything. She was arguing with fate, not me.

Slumped over the table, my father didn't have enough strength even to hold his fork. White beard bristles covered his gaunt face. His once-bright steady eyes sagged and blinked, straining to stay open.

We were all trying not to think about what would happen next.

My older brother Frank barked at me, "Help Dad out with his fork."

"Here, Dad," I said, as I twirled a fork of pasta up to his mouth. He opened and attempted to chew, but couldn't.

"Help him, Mike," said my brother again.

"Would you shut up," I whispered sternly. I tried again to hold the fork up to his mouth.

"I can't," my father replied bleakly, his eyes shutting. His chin dropped down into his chest. His body had given out. He slumped over to one side.

We jumped to help him. Frank got to him first.

Frank and I carried his six-foot one-inch body over to the couch, Frank giving me directions the whole time. Despite the fact that my father knew he was dying, he was smiling and serene. He started to sing "That's Life" weakly, but audibly. His eyes were closed.

"Riding high in April, then you're shot down in May."

As I stroked his hand, tears falling down my face, he continued singing to me, his voice getting quieter.

Then he stopped singing, smiled, opened his eyes wide and said, "Don't worry, kid. It's okay. Everything is okay." After a lifetime of not understanding each other, we had come to terms.

Now his singing faded to a whisper and then only to a slight hum. I continued stroking his thin gray hair.

Then he drifted off into a deep coma.

\#

Now at the hospital, maybe twelve hours later, he emerged from the coma. He said that an illuminated oval portrait of his family pulled him out. He followed its light until he awoke.

"Now I want to say a few things." The fatigue and morphine made his eyes bulbous and inflamed. He looked like an Old Testament prophet. My mother sat beside him. My brother, my two sisters and their husbands and I gathered around him.

"Your mother," he continued, holding her hand, "she should be put up in a closet." We all laughed. Of course, he meant, "Put up on a pedestal."

"When we first got married," he said, "your mother wanted sex all of the time."

"Frank!" my mother yelled, "what the hell are you talking about?" He never talked about sex. This was a man who, when he caught me masturbating in the bathroom unexpectedly, exclaimed, "You have to learn to control yourself, dammit."

"My penis was too small," he said. My brother and two sisters were now doubled over in hysterics.

"Frank that's enough now. Seriously. If you don't stop this, I'm going to smother you with a pillow," said my mother. Now the room was shaking with laughter.

Ignoring her, he continued, "I've always had a small penis."

Now a roar of hilarity brought the nurse to the room to see if everything was okay.

My brother waved her away. "It's okay," he said.

"What I am trying to say is that we stuck with it. Even with my small penis, I stuck it up there as far as I could."

My mother had tears coming down her face, as she choked with laughter.

"Your penis was perfect. It wasn't small. I can't believe how stupid you are," she said.

Now my father, a plain-speaking man, spoke like a visionary poet. He said that love is the key to living a good life. That love binds us to the circle of life, to God. He kept referring to what he called the "Sequence of Events."

He spoke for another hour and then became sleepy. The doctors suggested that we let him rest, so we each took turns saying goodbye. We all knew this was goodbye forever.

To my brother, the Wall Street trader, he said, "You'll always find a way. You're like the sky, you won't stop."

I couldn't hear what he said to my sisters. He spoke quietly to each of them, pulling them in closely.

To me he said, "No matter where you go, here or on Mars, there'll never be anyone like you." Now that he wasn't going to be around, he left all of his secrets to us.

Then he asked us all to leave so he could talk to my mother. We all watched from the other side of the glass window outside his room. He held her hand and they talked for a few minutes alone.

When we returned to his bedside, he had stopped talking. He started to hum again. He had worn himself out.

After a few seconds, even the humming trailed off.

He smiled and became silent.

Soon he fell back into a coma. During the night, his breath grew more and more shallow. He died at 4 the next morning.

The Mountain Man

For our honeymoon, Arielle and I went to Italy. Our plan was to land in Naples, take a boat ride to Salerno across the bay where we'd mainly stay, then make excursions to the surrounding towns and cities.

Our first night in Salerno, we got lost trying to find the restaurant listed in our guide. One left turn too many, we stumbled upon a dimly lit and modest-looking restaurant. It looked perfect: rustic, a diamond in the rough. It was a neighborhood place — there were only a few people eating and quietly talking.

It wasn't too different from neighborhood restaurants in any borough of New York City. If we closed our eyes we'd be back home. They spoke the shades of dialect you'd hear in New York City. As we sat down, Dean Martin's "Under the Bridges of Paris" played overhead. All night we heard Dean Martin.

We ordered our food.

As we talked, a man one table away hearing us speak English asked us where we were from. He spoke English well; I assumed he was German. When I said we were from New York, he was impressed.

"Wow — you are from New York, yes?"

"Yes, New York City," I said.

"You must be very special, yes?" he asked, "Maybe a movie star or a musician."

"Yes," I said, "I am a musician." Having a conversation across two tables was getting difficult so I asked him to join us. He agreed and brought his drink to our table.

"My name is Stefano," he said. He had long, straggly hair and glasses. He was about six feet tall and bulky, but very gentle looking.

"Where are you from?" I asked.

"I am from Cremona," he said, "the hometown of Stradivari."

Surprised I said, "Now that's impressive." Instrument making had been pioneered in Cremona.

"There is a lot of history in my town, this is true. But you are from New York!" Wherever you go in this world, people are impressed you're from New York City. I didn't tell him I'm from Queens.

Stefano explained that he was on his way to the island of Favignana in Sicily to meet his wife and daughter on vacation.

"That sounds exciting. I'd love to go to Sicily," I said. "My mother's family is from Sicily." I saw the island of Favignana in my mind, separated from Sicily only by the brilliant blue waters of the Mediterranean Sea. There is a great migration of tuna that passes Favignana and moves on toward Africa. It is, or was, the source of the island's main economy and culture.

"You are a real Italian," he said. "I'm not looking forward to it. I don't like the heat in the south and I don't like the sea."

He pouted when he spoke.

"I am from the North. I am a mountain man. I like cool weather and trees. This is too humid."

"Are you going fishing?" Arielle asked. She said that she loved the hot weather and the water in Naples.

"Yes," he said. "I don't want to but my wife's family likes to fish and to swim in the sea. Imagine swimming in the same place you eat? For me, it is hell." He winced and shook his head and said, "This is like a foreign country for me."

"It's strange you say that," I said, smiling, "I look around and hear the accents, see the faces, hear the music, smell the food, and it feels like home."

In perfect English, Stefano said, quietly now, "Half the time, I can't understand these people."

He said he had heard me trying to speak Italian. "It's not so bad," he said, trying to be nice. He leaned in close to me and said "But they don't speak Italian correctly."

"I can manage unless they speak too rapidly. I need a dictionary handy."

"Do you speak Italian in New York City?" he asked.

"No — never." I explained that I studied Italian in school and although my mother's parents spoke the Sicilian dialect, they only used it when they didn't want us to understand them.

"That sounds terrible," Stefano said. "I would never be able to understand them."

"I know. Just imagine how I felt." I explained that when I tried to use my school-learned Italian to talk to my grandfather I always struggled. And he teased me, calling me *Il Professore*. Reads books, doesn't know anything.

Stefano said, "Of course; it was the dialect."

"Do you speak a dialect in Cremona?" I asked.

"Yes — I love our dialect and our songs."

"Are they different from Neapolitan songs?"

He looked at me sternly. "Very different."

I asked him if the curse words were the same.

"Some," he said and laughed.

We exchanged a few curses. I told him the curses I remembered my grandfather saying. He kept looking around and laughing, hoping no one could hear us. The curse that made him double over in laughter was *minchia tu sorde* which means "dickhead, are you deaf?" He kept asking me to repeat it and then kept pleading with me to say it more quietly. It was like I was tickling him.

We finished our meal and Stefano said he had to retire early; he was taking an early boat ride to Sicily.

After Stefano left, Arielle said to me, "If I didn't know better, I would say that you're more Italian than he is."

Magic Egg

Just married, my wife Arielle and I landed in Naples, taking a train directly to the countryside in Pompeii.

In Pompeii we met a man trying to sell us tours. Pushing him off I said, "No thank you, we're here for our *luna di miele*," our honeymoon. As happened often during this vacation, he looked at me, heard my corrupted Italian, and asked me if I was Italian.

"*Tu sei Italiano, si?*"

"Yes, of course I am." I told him. Then we began our conversation in Italian and English with a lot of hand gestures.

I explained that my father's family was from Sala Consilina. He knew the town, of course. When Italians confirmed that I had an Italian heritage, they treated me slightly more like a countryman than a tourist. Southern Italians had connections to America; many of their cousins, fathers, uncles, and sisters had migrated to America over the past hundred years or so. Some of them had even lived in America, learned English and had moved back.

"You are on your *luna di miele*?" he asked again, just to make sure. He clasped his hands in prayer to bless the occasion.

I said, "Yes, we're on our honeymoon."

He told us he had a farm and began making elaborate animal sounds, sucking his teeth and mewing.

We weren't sure where he was going with this.

"*Va bene,*" I said. That's good.

He said he had rabbits, using his index fingers to describe the ears. He also had pigs, he said, snorting and pacing back and forth.

We watched him in utter amazement.

Then, he pointed his elbows out and began making sounds: coo ro coo, coo ro coo. He had a chicken that laid special eggs.

Now we started to laugh.

"My farm is in the valley," he continued, explaining that the soil was very rich. From his mixed English and Italian I understood that because his home was in the valley, vegetables and other plants grew big and animals were healthy and fat.

"On this farm," he said, now gesturing wildly with his hands, "I have a chicken that lays big a' eggs, very big a' eggs that are potent." His hands were wide apart, demonstrating the size. These eggs must have been as big as children.

Watching him move around, we waited for what was going to come next.

"I can give you one of these eggs," he said, "for your *luna di miele.* When you eat a' this egg you can a' to fuck like boom boom boom!" he said, punching his right fist into his left hand.

He continued, undaunted by the look of astonishment on our faces.

"When you eat a' these egg in a' the morning you can a' to fuck like boom boom boom, like a Vesuvius, you explode to make the babies."

We didn't say anything.

After a pause, he asked, "Where are you staying?"

We pointed at the hotel right across the street. The Vesuvio.

"*Domani*, I bring a' the egg for you. You can to eat it and then to make a' the love."

Arielle asked, "What time will you be here?"

He said he would set up his stand at 9:00 a.m. and stay until the afternoon.

In the hotel that night I read for a while then rolled over and went to sleep.

Next day, Arielle jumped out of bed early. She rushed to get dressed and get me out of bed. We went to see our friend, the Pompeian farmer with the magic eggs.

Practically running down the street, my shoes untied, Arielle still tucking in her tank top, we finally got to where his stand had been.

But he wasn't there.

Arielle looked disappointed. I was somewhat relieved. I was worried that the egg would make my head explode, or my eyes would fall out. Maybe it was some kind of village witchcraft. Was it something invented by Italian sorceresses to get rid of a horrible husband? But I wasn't so bad. At least not yet — we'd only just got married. We were on our *luna di miele*.

During our walk back to the hotel room, we saw an old man playing a guitar and singing on the street. We slowed down a bit as we approached him.

I was in a fog, so I didn't completely hear and see him at first. Then I noticed the man looked like my mother's Uncle Rudy. He was rail thin and had dark, bony hands. His face was wrinkled.

Fiercely emerging from his old face with volcanic intensity was his gigantic nose. I began to actually hear the song — it was *Malafemmena*, a song I had grown up with. I had played this song many times for Arielle.

Arielle looked at me as if I'd asked the man to play it. I just shrugged and asked, "Isn't life ironic sometimes?"

Now we made a full stop and listened.

The old Neapolitan sang the song sweetly, not having to belt or wrestle with it. Though the song bemoans a man's unrequited love for a beautiful though devilish woman, he sang it softly and sadly, as if whispering it in your ear, telling you a secret. His strong hands strummed the guitar powerfully.

The old man's song was both sweet and ancient; listening to it was a journey in itself. Although not an old song itself, *Malafemmena* contained hundreds of years of Neapolitan music, harking back even to the Arab invaders who brought their musical traditions to southern Italy. The lyrics were out of a tradition — not unlike the many blues, country and jazz songs that describe a broken heart, an unfaithful lover and the loss of love.

Arielle and I walked away from the man and went back to our hotel room.

We didn't need any magic eggs.

Escape from Pompeii

Leaving Pompeii, we took a taxi to the train station only ten blocks away. It was easier than lugging our bags.

When we got into the cab, the driver spoke to me in dialect. If I understood correctly, he said he was going to pick up another fare and take them to the Pompeii station too.

He asked me if I understood.

I said, "*Credo di ci.*" I think so.

He laughed. My wife, Arielle, trusted that I knew what I was doing.

The driver looked like a cross between Jimmy Durante and Popeye. His name was Luigi. He was about seventy, short and muscular. He wore thick glasses that made his eyes bulge. I was sure he couldn't see too well, if at all.

We drove about fifteen blocks out of the way to pick up the other fare. He swerved into oncoming cars, not because he was trying to hit them but because he couldn't see them. He hit the side-view mirror of a car with a woman driver and two kids then yelled at them, "*Minchia tu sorde!*" Shut up you dickhead. I turned to Arielle and told her that my grandfather used to say that.

"Didn't your grandfather speak Sicilian?" she asked.

"I guess they curse the same."

He finally pulled into a gravel driveway, got out of the car and asked us to wait. He walked to a small business office about twenty yards away and then walked back to the car. A few minutes later two men hauling luggage in light brown, shiny European suits walked toward the car. They were friendly, smiling, and spoke English.

"Luigi, come stai?" the taller one asked the cab driver. Luigi seemed happy to see them like they were old friends. They all shook hands.

When the two men got into the car, they told us that they worked for a Brazilian manufacturing company with a plant in Pompeii that made sportswear for soccer teams and other sports.

As he pulled out of the driveway, Luigi said, *"Shamonie."* Let's go. "Now we go to the Naples Station. Twenty dollars each."

I looked at the Brazilian guys.

Luigi kept driving.

"Did he say we're going to the Naples Station?" I asked. They seemed to understand him better than I did.

"Yes," they said, smiling. I suspected this was a ruse that Luigi had pulled before. Maybe the Brazilians were in on it, maybe not.

"I never said I agreed to go to the Naples Station," I said. "We only want to go to the Pompeii Station. That's a ten-dollar ride."

Luigi made a big fuss, cursing, thrusting his hands wildly as if to shake off an evil spell. He didn't look at me though, not even through the rear-view mirror.

"Disgraziato, ingrato," he said, cursing me, calling me ungrateful. He complained that he tried to arrange this ride for all of us as a convenience. I was ungrateful and didn't appreciate his gesture.

As I sat and listened to his rant, Arielle and I laughed with the Brazilians. Luigi's audacity was so transparent it was comical. It was a performance.

Now, having driven about three miles, Luigi kept slamming his hands on the steering wheel. It seemed that we were going to Naples no matter what.

I thought to myself, well, here we are, the luggage is in the trunk, this guy is a maniac and we'll at least have a story to tell — if we survive the ride.

I said aloud, "Okay, *andiamo a Napoli.*" Let's go to Naples. The Brazilians clapped and a big smile broke out on Luigi's face. Though he stopped banging on the steering wheel, his driving remained out of control.

The Brazilians told us when they come to their Pompeii office, they always call Luigi.

"But aren't you afraid he can't see and can't drive?" I asked.

"Have you seen the other drivers in Italy?"

As Luigi floored the pedal and steered with his fingertips, he handed us a picture of his Brazilian girlfriend with his left hand, reaching over the seat. He had apparently shown it to the Brazilians previously. They teased him saying that she was too old for him. She wasn't more than twenty-five. Wearing an outrageous sexy costume, she looked like a dancer.

Luigi said he had many girlfriends.

I joked about whether or not he used Viagra. I said that Luigi probably drank a potion mixed with ash from Pompeii to get his mythic potency. Or maybe he ate magic eggs. Maybe they all ate magic eggs in Pompeii.

We all laughed, even Luigi.

He now turned almost fully around to look at us, completely disregarding the road, his arms somehow still holding the wheel. Then he handed us another photo out of his pile of 11 by 14-inch pictures. It was an image of Vesuvius covered in plastic — like a placemat at a pizza restaurant. He then pointed to the Virgin Mary pendant he had hanging on his rear-view mirror saying something about how Mary saves the Pompeiians from devastation every day. He made the sign of the cross; the Brazilians did too. I looked at Arielle and we made the sign of the cross so as not to offend anyone.

Luigi thanked the Blessed Virgin for allowing us to safely leave Pompeii. He said the Hail Mary in his dialect. He didn't offer a prayer to save us from his driving.

Everyone quieted and bowed their heads.

When he finished, we started talking again about his beautiful and sexy Brazilian girlfriend.

We then drove into Naples; Luigi dropped the Brazilians off first.

At this point, he had warmed up to us and now considered Arielle and me his friends.

He pulled out a cassette of Neapolitan songs and began playing the song *Piscatore 'e Pusilleco*, the Fishermen of Pusilleco.

I translated his Italian for Arielle.

"I like how Claudio Villa sings this song," he said. "It's from the heart," he added, pointing to his chest.

He then paused.

Now hardly looking at the road he said, "When I was a young man, I had one true love." He pointed his index finger into the air to emphasize the number one.

"But I became a sailor and went to the sea," he said. Then he stopped talking. His face dropped.

"When I came back to Pompeii, she'd married another man who'd taken her north." He cursed the fact that he'd left her and said that this explained his love of young women; he was trying to get back to her, his long lost Maria. He then became sullen and quietly sang along with the song.

When the song ended, Luigi just looked straight ahead, not talking to us at all. We had been invited into his heart and were friends forever. We knew his secret.

He insisted on driving us directly to the hotel where we were staying. Gentle as a lamb, he stepped out of the car and before I could open the door, he opened it for us and unloaded our luggage.

He handed me the cassette of Neapolitan songs by Claudio Villa.

I said no, it was okay, he didn't have to give it to me.

He said that I was Neapolitan and should know the songs of my countrymen.

I agreed and offered him a few dollars extra.

No, he said. I could only give him twenty dollars like we agreed — not a cent more. He managed to wheel and deal me anyway despite his offer of friendship.

He hugged Arielle and me. He seemed even a little choked up like we were his children or his relatives. He had tears running down his cheeks.

We said goodbye and told him that when we were back in Pompeii we would look him up.

He handed me his private card and got back into his car, waving goodbye.

I hoped that he'd make it back.

Addio Fiorito

My father told me that the Fiorito name was common in the region around Naples. Even though Arielle and I were on our honeymoon, this was also a personal journey. Though my father was born in downtown Manhattan, I felt that I was making a pilgrimage to the land of my ancestors.

Neapolitans looked like my relatives: The policeman looked like my mother's Uncle Rudy; he was short, dark and burly. The ticket clerk looked like Aunt Dolly; she had red hair, bright blue eyes and a broad smile. The street sweeper looked like cousin Tutti; tall, handsome, a mop of black wavy hair on his head. Some of them even looked like me. Their hands were square and muscular, but not big. Their hair was dark and curly. They had extraordinary noses: wide, with big nostrils. But their noses were handsome.

Everywhere we went, I repeated my stories to restaurant owners, store clerks, people on the street — really anyone who'd listen. People would look at me funny at first. "You are from this area, no?" they'd ask.

"My father's grandfather was from Sala Consilina," I'd answer, giving them the family's migration story to New York City.

A restaurant owner in Naples, who said he worked in New York City many years earlier, spoke at length about Sala Consilina and the Fiorito name.

"It's a common name in Naples," he said, "but especially in Sala Consilina." The Neapolitan sun bore down on us as we talked, even though it was after 3:00 p.m. If you didn't eat by noon, you had to wait until 3:00 p.m. to eat. Only tourists walked the streets during the day in Naples, our glossy guidebooks glaring in the Neapolitan sun. The sun finally yielded, but was still strong enough to make us retreat to the shade, underneath an umbrella.

"Really? You know this for sure?" I asked pathetically, like a man searching for a father who'd abandoned him as a child.

"Of course," he said, as a moped roared by.

I hadn't done any research prior to coming to Naples. After all, this was our honeymoon, not a National Geographic assignment. I could have looked up the Fiorito name and arranged planned meetings with people. I thought I would wing it instead and just see what happened.

In Salerno, I kept searching the mailboxes to see if I'd see the name Fiorito. I'd open one of the heavy iron-gated doors and look up and down the list of names. No Fioritos. I saw Gallos, Rubinos, Marinos, and other names I can't remember, but no Fioritos.

Arielle and I fell in love with Salerno. Unlike Naples, Capri, and Sorrento, Salerno was hardly a tourist city. If there were tourists they seemed mostly Italian. Salerno streets were narrow and paved with stone. The age of the apartment buildings ranged by hundreds of years and they were made of different materials; some darker shades of stone, some bone white and shining. Dressed in pearls and sunglasses, people emerged from these old cave-like structures and stepped into fancy Italian sports cars.

One night, we got lost trying to find a restaurant recommended by a guidebook. Instead we found another restaurant — very small, very modest looking. We ordered eggplants, sopressata, salamis, ciabatta breads and wine. The food was delicious; the servings generous. Of course I went through my usual speech about my father's family.

"Fiorito?" the waitress said, "Yes, I know the name; it's very common in this region."

I looked at her yearningly, as if wanting her to produce a few of them here and now for me. I'd love to meet them, see if we looked alike, and find out if they had relatives who went to America. Of course they would. I tried my best to speak in Italian, using a dictionary when I didn't know the word — which was often. In the end we went back to that restaurant a few times. We discovered that most everyone in the restaurant was related. The cook was the waitress's husband and the man who worked the brick oven was their son.

Ironically, the one time in my life when more than one person commented on the name Fiorito was when I lived in Berkeley, California. I worked on the retail floor of a computer store. Men old enough to have been in World War II would come in to purchase computers and accessories. They all looked the same to me: tall, graying, and wearing baseball caps inscribed with the names of their military divisions. When they saw my name tag they'd ask, "Are you related to Ted Fiorito, the bandleader?"

No, I'd reply. I'd known of him but I wasn't related to him. My father often talked about Ted Fiorito, a less-popular Guy

Lombardo who performed for the troops around the country. His performances were also broadcast on the military radio networks so his name was known among this population.

We rented a car to make a trip to Sala Consilina. It was an hour's drive outside of Naples. Along the way, we passed Teggiano, the town my friend Roberto is from. Arielle and I waved "hello" as we drove by. Maybe a hundred years earlier, our ancestors had argued over a bale of hay. Maybe they were at war. It would remain a mystery.

I was expecting Sala Consilina to be a poor town. After all, why would our family have left if they had lived comfortably? As we drove, there were signs to Eboli on the highway. I thought about "Christ Stopped at Eboli" written during World War II by Carlo Levi. Because he was an intellectual — an artist — Levi was banished to the worst possible place in Italy that Mussolini could send him.

Levi describes the poverty, illiteracy, and superstition that the Southern Italians demonstrated. Though they were Italians too, they were described as being from the third world. The title implies that European civilization never made it to Eboli and the towns south of it.

"Christ Stopped at Eboli" inspired reform in Italy and created a movement to address inequity in the South. As I drove along the highway, I felt a pain in my stomach imagining my ancestors who had lived so close to this border where civilization ended.

This realization made me quiet during the ride. This and the idea that it felt like this was the closest I had been to my father in the twenty years since he died. I felt like I was going to visit him. I was also nervous that my already fledgling Italian would crumble when confronted with an even more exotic dialect.

When we arrived in Sala Consilina it was more an affluent mountain town than a village of muddy huts and shoeless people. We'd learned that a Fiat factory had opened in Sala Consilina, part of the movement to enrich the South's economy. There weren't any broken-down shacks or littered roads.

It looked more like a northern Californian town — except some of the homes were from the fifteenth century and even older. As we drove up a ridge that looked over the valley, some of the homes had flags hanging from their windows. They looked like the flags you'd see at the horse races in Siena. Whatever poverty had plagued this town had been lifted.

We stopped to get a coffee at a café. I was afraid to talk, hoping they wouldn't begin to rattle off words I couldn't understand. I used few words to order and the waiter answered sparingly. He seemed cautious as if to say, "Oh no, another American coming to find his roots, maybe make claim to his great-great-great-grandfather's land." They probably didn't get a lot of strangers in this town.

We walked along the main street with boutiques that sold hats, clothes, and confections.

I didn't ask anyone about the name Fiorito. No one seemed interested in talking to us and I was feeling shy or too nervous to talk to anyone.

We stopped to get gas on the edge of the town. The gas station attendant — an old man who looked like me — was very friendly. He acted as if we were the only people he had seen in days. I had my usual conversation with him. He said, yes, there were many Fioritos in this region. He said he was not from Sala Consilina, but was from another town over the hills. He pointed to it, gesturing for me to follow his finger to see his hometown. He said that we were still *paese*, countrymen.

We drove up and down the streets of Sala Consilina but there wasn't anywhere to go that wasn't a restaurant or a shop so we drove back to Salerno before sunset.

We left Salerno and Sala Consilina, saying goodbye to imagined relatives I never knew. We took the train to Naples so we could get to the airport early the next morning. I said goodbye to my father, knowing he'd be proud that I went to visit the town he talked so much about when I was a kid. I wished I could have told him that it wasn't poor anymore; these people had disposable cash to buy funny hats and eat expensive candy.

In Naples we stayed at a hotel near the train station, which turned out to be an awful neighborhood with littered streets and rakish characters. It reminded me of the old Times Square.

But here we were back in Naples — a city I had always imagined but never thought I'd visit.

For our last night out on our honeymoon, we took a cab ride to a nicer part of town to eat dinner and enjoy the grandeur of Vesuvius looming in the sky. We left the hotel and walked to the ATM to get money for the evening.

And standing before us, in all of its glory, was a dreary-looking watch shop. Its windows were dirty and the watches on display didn't look any cleaner. The store was gated. The shop's name was written across the awning unimpressively. The name wasn't written in neon; it was displayed more like a five-and-dime sign. But I looked proudly. My search was over. In bold and powerful letters for all of the prostitutes, drug dealers and riff raff to see was our family name, "Fiorito," practically exploding onto the street.

I told Arielle I was kind of happy it was closed. I didn't want to go in there. Maybe behind the counter some man who only looked like my father would be rude to me. He wouldn't recognize me as I looked brokenheartedly at him. I couldn't bear it. I would just have to say goodbye to Naples and goodbye to my father one more time. For now.

Crossroads

"So, you're looking to give your music a charge?" says the devil. Her squinty eyes sparkle with excitement.

"That's why I'm here, lady. Look, I am going to die young and I want to make music that's never been heard before – something different," replies Walden Robert Cassato. He took this trip to the Dockery Plantation, like the bluesmen before him, to make a deal with the devil. What he didn't know was that the devil was a pretty woman. At least this one was.

"You guys come to me as if I can perform magic."

"Isn't that what you do?"

"I'm not a beautician and I don't do miracles," she says gesturing at his balding head and pointing to his paunch.

He feels self-conscious, especially because she's so beautiful. Her green eyes look like gems against her long black hair. Not only is the devil a woman, he thinks, but she wears leather too.

"You know what's on the table?" she asks, curving her full red lips as she speaks.

"My soul," he answers flatly.

"Yes, your soul which in your case is somewhat forthcoming since you're on the express train."

Rolling his eyes, he says, "Okay – what do I need to do?"

"Sign this," she says, pulling out a long scroll, with his name inked on the parchment.

He reads through it. In return for his eternal soul, he'll be bestowed with outstanding musical and performing ability. He reads the disclaimers at the bottom.

"What's this about having to wear a toupee and change my name to Bobby Darin?" he says frowning.

"Look kid, you're short, you're bald, you're ugly, you have a funny name and you have a big Italian nose. Need I say more?"

"I just want to sing like no one has before."

"I understand, but like I said, I don't do miracles. I'm kind of like a job counselor, too. Believe me, it's not what I want to do, but I've got to protect my investment."

He pauses, biting his lip.

"Look, it worked for Tony Bennett."

"Bennett's bald?"

"And he changed his name too. Part of the contract."

"I can't believe that Bennett is bald too," he says.

"Do you think that a balding man with a nose like a parrot could make it in the entertainment world?"

"Besides, I thought you only did blues singers."

"I've done them all, honey. You name it."

"What about Sinatra?"

"The skinny boy from Hoboken with the big voice? Who do you think put the wind in his lungs?"

"Sinatra doesn't wear a toupee."

"Take another look, kid. His hair's been thinning since his early days with Dorsey."

"What was his name before?"

"We made an exception in his case. You don't know what it's like dealing with that Dolly, his mother. What's done is done and I'll never let that happen again."

He looks down at the contract.

"What's it going to be?" she asks, taking the contract back.

"It's just that ..."

She starts rolling up the contract.

He grabs it from her.

"Okay, okay. I'll do it."

Reaching out to slash his finger with a razor, she obtains his fingerprint in blood on the contract. It's done.

Performing at the Copacabana, many years later, Bobby Darin is singing his career blazing smash hit "Beyond the Sea" to an enthralled audience. Despite his swaying and dancing, his toupee grips tight on his head. He's thin as a rail, like his idol Sinatra. The pretty devil didn't take away his paunch – that was his doing. As he sings, his nose doesn't look so big either. He sings with elegance and grace, his arms gesturing outward as if launching each verse. His fingers snap in time to the music.

Backstage in the dressing room after the show, Darin looks at himself in the mirror.

He takes the toupee off.

I'm still the same schlemiel that I was before when I take this damned toupee off. I've conquered the industry, just like the devil said I would. I've done it all: ballads, rock 'n' roll, and Carnegie Hall. She's held her part of the bargain.

In the mirror, his nose seems to grow larger. Looking down at his belly, it seems to protrude slightly. From the continuous nights of performing, and even working on movie sets, his eyes look weary.

I look like a bald, schlumpy old man.

He puts the toupee back on and slowly he transforms before his own eyes, returning back to his handsomer self.

Standing at the crossroads outside the Dockery Plantation, Darin waits for the pretty devil to materialize.

"So, did you come back to thank me," she says, suddenly appearing behind him. He turns around to face her. He smells her perfume. It's musky, sensuous.

"A kiss will do," she says, flashing her green eyes at him. "Even with your toupee off, you have a little charm left from all of your success."

He suddenly feels shy.

"Well, I'll tell you why I've come back," he says, trying to pull himself from the sway of her beauty.

"I've come back to tell you that I don't want any of this any longer."

He looks at her. She is silent.

"I mean, you held your part of the bargain, this is true, but after all of these years now, I don't want any of this. Here I am singing these ridiculous songs to people drinking cocktails."

Her face is saying, "Look, I'm the devil, do you think I give a shit?"

"There's a war in Vietnam, people are starving here in our own country. I don't want to be a phony anymore. I want to sing peace songs. And I don't want to wear this toupee," he says shaking the ragged tuft in his hands.

"So sing peace songs – be my guest. What do you want from me?" Her face wrinkles in disgust.

He tries to ignore it. "Can I sing peace songs without my toupee? I want to be real."

"You can," she says slyly, "but they will likely be flat and boring. Even your peace-mongers don't want to look at an ugly protest singer. I can tell you that Dylan's hair is the real thing. He doesn't need my help; he's already got enough of the devil in him."

"So I'll be a failure without it?" he asks, like a little boy asking his mother for permission to leave the dinner table.

She doesn't answer.

"What about my soul? I gave my soul to you."

"Yes, but according to the contract, there's a minor stipulation about wearing a toupee."

"But I don't want to wear it anymore," he says like a whining baby.

"A deal's a deal. I kept my part; even you agreed."

"Well, I'm not going to wear it. How can I be free when I hide behind a toupee?" He stomps his foot down.

"Honey, don't lecture me on freedom, please," she says, lighting a cigarette.

Darin returns to California, showing his bald head to the world.

He sells everything he owns, gives his money away to charity and moves into a small house by the ocean.

At his next show, he gets up in front of the audience and begins playing peace songs on his acoustic guitar. No band. He is stationary when he performs. He looks austere and determined to save the world.

The audience is silent.

No one is cheering. Are they excited to hear my new songs of freedom? Do I have to prance around like a buffoon to make people enjoy my music? What about music for its own sake, or better yet, music for peace?

By the time the show is over, the auditorium is nearly empty.

A woman with a flower in her hair approaches him after the show. She is very stoned. She's a groupie.

"That was amazing, man," she says, blinking, her speech slow and exaggerated.

"You like the songs?"

"You're beautiful, man. Your songs are like pretty doves touching everyone in the universe."

He doesn't know exactly what that means.

"Which song did you like best?"

"Hey man, I like them all. Especially the one about the dove."

"I don't have a song about a dove."

She reaches down and touches his groin.

He backs up.

"Hey, why'd you do that?"

"You're beautiful, man."

"What about my music? Goddamn! Would you touch Dylan's groin?"

"Dylan's beautiful man – I would eat my brain for him if he asked me to. I love Dylan. He's so righteous."

Disgusted, he leaves the woman and walks back to his dressing room.

He pulls the toupee out of a red shoebox that he carries around and places it on his head.

It seems to light up his face immediately.

"What is it with this thing? Is it me or the wig that makes the music?"

His reflection doesn't answer.

"Dylan must have a wig. That ball of fur on his head can't be real. Besides where does he get those inspired lyrics. The devil was lying to me just to make me jealous. Why can't I write a song like Blowing in the Wind"?

He starts singing "Blowing in the Wind" in the mirror.

The groupie wasn't even referring to my song, he thinks, noting the mention of the white dove in the verse. I can't even convince the maniacs that I'm a bona-fide protest singer. But I do look better in the toupee. I even sound better. This confounded spell only works with the wig, it's true. All I want is to save the world, but I can't have that and spread my songs of peace. They just won't have me; I'm no good without the piece, let's face it. He adjusts the toupee, so it looks perfect, straps his guitar around his neck and begins singing.

He's pleased with his song sung with the wig on, trying to convince himself that Dylan also wears a wig.

No More Pork Chops

"Listen to this Theo," I say, playing Wingy Manone's 1928 collection. Suddenly the music sounds corny even to me, like a Dixieland band crumbling into a pile of disjointed honks and shrieks.

"Take it off," he says, stepping towards the iPod player. I reach out to turn the music off.

"I hate it," he says. "Turn it off."

I turn it off.

It's not so much his rejection of this particular song that pisses me off; it's his waving off an entire era of music. I want to talk about Wingy Manone, tell him the story of how Wingy got his name; that he was a one-armed phenomenon, but it seems pointless now.

"What should I put on?"

"Don't put on that shit."

I don't put on anything.

I think to myself that he's going to regret this behavior someday. I understand regret. I was seventeen; I remember being an asshole to my father. Trying to shift gears, I ask Theo about dinner.

"What do you want to eat?"

"What do you have?"

"We have pork chops."

"I don't want pork chops."

"I texted you earlier asking what you wanted and you didn't answer so I bought pork chops."

"Can I get Chinese food?"

"No. I bought pork chops."

"Okay, I'll have pork chops."

As I fry the pork chops in the pan, I think about the way my father used to cook for me. He'd put a lot of care into making food, frequently turning the pork chops over, adding salt. He'd slice open the meat so he could look at it, making sure it wasn't pink. He grimaced, baring his teeth, as he forked the meat. Cooking required using your entire body. When he served it to me he'd search my face.

"Tases' good?"

"Tastes good," I'd say, eating my pork chop. He'd ask questions like, "You don't want no more pork chops?" or "You don't like it?" I'd laugh at him. He wasn't joking.

I'm making the chops like my dad did, stabbing them with my fork, turning them over on the plate. I slice the meat and peek inside to see if it's pink. My face wrinkles as I poke. You can't overdo it and you can't underdo it.

Proudly, I bring the plate to the table; the chops are hot, steam rising off the plate. It smells good. I feel useful.

I stare at him as he eats.

"How do you like them?" I ask.

"They're okay," he says, cutting a piece and then picking up his iPhone.

"Could you put the iPhone down?" I ask him about track practice.

"Wait," he says, distractedly. He pecks out a rapid message on his iPhone with his thumb.

"Please don't ask me to wait," I say.

"Hold on," he says, palming the phone with his left hand, forking up cut pieces of pork chop with his left hand.

I am somewhere between wanting to belt him on the nose and wanting to give him an embrace. The fact is I love every minute of the time he's with me. I don't get to see him every night any more. He stays with his mom more than half the time now, coming to me here and there, sometimes unannounced. I can hardly prepare for him. He's going to college next year; these are precious moments. I don't want to bicker the whole time.

"What?" he says now, picking up his head to look at me. He's ready to talk.

"What?" I repeat back, exasperated. He talks to me like I'm wasting his time.

He smirks.

"How are the chops?"

"Good, I said they're good."

"Have you had enough?"

"I'm still eating them."

"You don't want no more?" I say to him mimicking my father. He knows the routine. We repeat the routines that my father and I used to play out. Another one is "Where are your slippers?" My father would ask this all the time, as if the state of my feet had any bearing on the universe. Now I do the same thing to my son. I want his feet to be safe and warm. When he was a boy I would fluff up his covers before putting him to sleep. Even now, when he lies down to sleep, all six feet three of him, I jokingly still fluff up the covers. He doesn't mind the joke.

He finishes eating, there's a piece of pork chop left on the plate.

"Good?"

"I'm good," he says, going back to his iPhone.

I grab the plate, then take it into the kitchen.

After washing the dishes, I find him in the living room on the couch. Before I sit with him, I put the music back on shuffle. I can't help it that Wingy comes back on.

Theo rolls his eyes.

"Who is this?" he asks.

"Wingy Manone," I say. "New Orleans trumpet player with one arm."

"Him, okay," he says, which sounds slightly like "oh no, not him," but only slightly.

He kicks his big legs out on the couch, going over my lap. I push his legs away.

"Do you have to put your legs on top of me?"

He moves his legs away. They don't fit anywhere.

We look at each other and smile. Neither of us is supposed to enjoy this.

Broken

We'd been playing football catch in the park for hours. The sky above us was spotted with rippled lilac tinted clouds. As we ran back and forth, I never lost site of the church spire that needled the sky.

"I don't feel like playing anymore," my son Adam said, his eyes watery and sparkling. His wrinkled smile made him look older suddenly. He was fourteen.

"Come on," I insisted. Pointing to my watch, I added "Let's play for another thirty minutes." I pushed him to withstand the meanness of the world.

Adam looked at my watch with me, then our eyes met. He stared at me blankly.

"Who's the old man, now?" I said with a smirk. I often called him old man, as if to say if I can do it, you can do it.

Finally, his eyes softened and a broad grin broke across his face.

"I'm not the old man," he said.

Then he started trotting across the field for a pass. It was our way of communicating without words.

I cocked my arm back to launch a pass.

"Come on, old man, don't drop this one," I shouted, my voice echoed in the park. He ran faster and faster on the balls of his feet. The distant sounds of other children chittered in the background, like a swirl of birds.

At thirty-five, I was in great shape. I lifted weights a few times a week, jogged, and did yoga. I didn't yet know it, but I had reached my peak. Adam, on the other hand, was about to shoot past me in every way.

At home a week later, I heard a knock at the door. I wasn't expecting anyone.

"Who is it?" I asked.

No response. I opened the door. A young woman I didn't know handed me a manila envelope.

"You've been served," she said, coldly, then walked away. My ex-wife, Adam's mother, had sent a messenger, probably a law school friend, to deliver a child custody subpoena to me.

I took the envelope in a dream-like state, holding the package away from my body with my thumb and forefinger, like it was contaminated.

But the poison made contact with my skin. The moment I opened the door, the subpoena seemed to seep into my body. With a gush of wind my hair went a shade whiter, my bones became softer, like clay.

From then on, almost every time we saw each other, after school and on weekends, Adam and I played until the blue sky grew dark. I'd run until I could taste the sweat, like salted tears, leaking into the corners of my mouth.

Two years prior, I had remarried and now had a one year old child. While Adam's mother had perhaps worried that my attentions would divert to my new family, I knew they would not. But I had to prove to Adam that I would always be completely his father. He had to know it in every cell of his body. It didn't matter if it killed me.

Months later, we played catch in the park again. I could imagine lying down on the ground and looking up at the clouds until I vanished into mist.

But I didn't. I swallowed gusts of wind and ran with my son.

"Keep going," I said, pointing to where I would throw the ball, fifty yards away. I launched the ball; it sailed in the air, and he caught it just in the right spot. Unlike my life, which was unhinged and shaky, Adam's catches were solid, perfect. After a few hours of catch, my heart beat steadily, calming the jitters I felt inside. I pretended I was teaching him the endurance that life demands. But really, I was learning that lesson myself.

Throwing the ball over and over, night after night, I began to feel a knotted lump in my shoulder. Hurling long passes repeatedly ground down my weakening bones. Time heals young bones with blood and sleep. But this hurt wasn't going away. After finally going to the doctor, almost a year later, I learned that I had torn my rotator cuff and developed a few other tears in my shoulder. I also had progressive arthritis in my arms and creeping into my legs. The tighter I gripped, the more I fell apart.

Now the bickering with my ex-wife grew worse. With the court case in progress, I had to keep a record of how many days Adam stayed with me, how much extra I spent on him for sneakers, swimming goggles, miscellaneous items. It killed me that this upset him.

"I need to keep this," I said after buying him sneakers, taking the receipt out of the shopping bag.

"Why? What if I need to exchange them?"

"I'll go with you. I have to keep track of these things now." I felt cruel saying it, but I didn't see how I could avoid telling him. He had to know.

"Why?"

"You know what's going on, right?" I asked.

"Mom's not going to do anything."

"She's already doing something. Don't you understand?"

He did not want to understand. It cut him deeply.

When it was all over, I showed him the court decision papers, explaining that she had lost the case. I owed her minor child support payment adjustments, but she did not win child custody. It was unfounded; Adam lived with me half of the time anyway.

"I don't know what this means," he said.

"Look here," I said, pointing to the paragraph that read "full custody request denied."

He took another look at the papers. Then he looked at me.

"When did you and mom get married?" he asked, seeing that his birthday came only three months after the marriage date. He caught me by surprise. This was a conversation that had waited fifteen years.

"Mom was pregnant when we married," I said. I wouldn't lie to him.

He couldn't speak, his lips moved silently. He grew pale, as if fading from the world.

"Look, when Mom was pregnant, I was scared shitless. I didn't want to be a dad."

"That's supposed to make me feel better?"

"You don't understand. I didn't want a child, a son." This was coming out all wrong. My heart spewed words before my brain could intercept them. "And then you came along. You came along and I fell in love with you, completely. You taught me how to be a father," I said, holding back tears. He didn't want me to cry.

Adam didn't talk to me for a few weeks.

I held back telling him that his mom's interest in me had mainly revolved around her getting U.S. citizenship. At the time I met her, she was in the U.S. with an expired Visa only. After she obtained her citizenship her affections for me, which had never been strong, rapidly faded.

Like when spring returns, miraculously, one day he started speaking to me again. Hearing his words was like feeling sunshine on my face after a terrible winter.

Years later, now eighteen, he stood six foot three — his body filled out from high school swimming and track. Adam grew tall like my father. We had become father and son to each other.

"Watch out, Dad," Adam said, holding onto my arm, as we crossed the street. The nearest car more than a block away.

"I see the car," I said. "I'm not blind and senile — yet."

Even though I was annoyed, his concern comforted me.

He put his arm around me, cloaking me. I could tell it made him feel good to tower over me, to pull and push me at will. The taller he grew, the more I shrank, as if our life forces were feeding into each other. Until then, it had never occurred to me that I had always been short, but against his height that was inescapably clear.

And he grew in other ways.

For the past three years, Adam wouldn't even look at his little brother, Samer. Now, when Samer ran to Adam when he walked in the door, Adam embraced Samer the way I held him as a boy, his arm wrapped around his waist, patting his back.

One night, Adam lay in bed with me while I read Samer to sleep. The three of us, with me in the middle. Samer curled up to Adam, tucked in his armpit.

"Did you read to me like that?" Adam asked, later.

"Of course," I said, "exactly the same."

"What did you read?"

"I read the same books to you."

It must be strange watching your father grow up another child, I thought. It's like watching a film of yourself as a child.

The next day in the park, Adam and Samer and I tossed the football around.

I lobbed the ball to Samer underhanded. He dropped it.

"Show your little brother how to catch the ball," I said to Adam. Adam instructed him, showing Samer how to catch with his hands, then pull the ball into his chest, like I once showed him.

Out of breath, we stood next to each other, father, big brother and little brother.

"I'm going to miss you when you go to college," I said to Adam, knowing that autumn would rush upon us all too soon. I dreaded that day, knowing there would be no way I could hold him back.

"I'll miss you, too," he replied.

"Will you come with me to Mary's parents on Christmas?" I asked. It had been on my mind for weeks now. Coming to my wife Mary's parent's house was like going to grandparents that didn't treat him like a grandchild. It had been hard for Adam to accept Mary's family and they didn't make it easier.

"Yes, I'll come," he said.

"Are you serious?" The fear of being apart had been swallowing me, a little bit at a time, like I was on a boat drifting further out to sea.

"Yes, I'm serious."

"What happened that now you're coming?"

"I was broken before," he said. "But I'm fixed now." He continued, "I'll come for Samer."

He motioned with his head for me to stop talking and to throw the ball, like I used to do to him. As he dashed across the field, Samer hopelessly chasing behind him, I fired a perfect arc thirty feet away.

Looking over his left shoulder, he guided the ball to land perfectly in his big cupped hands.

Please Don't Squeeze the Banana

While the African-American impact on jazz is recognized and well established, the contribution of Italian immigrants on jazz is not. Italians arrived in America playing mandolin, violin, guitar and piano. They brought traditions of Southern-Italian marching bands, opera and folk histories. Whether Neapolitan, Sicilian or Calabrese, they understood passion and romanticism in music. And the Italian propensity for humor and style contributed to the theater of early jazz. In addition to outstanding musicianship, Italian performers were also entertaining.

So why do these facts go unmentioned in many mainstream jazz documentaries and literature? Ken Burns, for example, neglects to mention the impact of Italians on jazz in his popular "Jazz" documentary. He makes one mention of Nick LaRocca suggesting that LaRocca was one of the white musicians who got on the jazz bandwagon only when jazz became popular. However, Burns doesn't mention that LaRocca wrote "Tiger Rag" and that he was one of the many influential New Orleans Sicilian musicians who forged jazz history. Even Louis Prima doesn't get a mention. Although Burns features Benny Goodman's version of "Sing, Sing, Sing," he never tells us that Prima wrote it. Burns disregards the great fount of Sicilian jazz musicians that came from New Orleans and never explores conditions that put them in the creative center of the development of jazz. Consequently, people like Wingy Manone, Sharkey Bonano, Leon Rappolo, John Signorelli, Ted Fiorito, Eddie Lang, Adrian Rollini, Sam Butera and countless other Italian-American artists who shaped the soul and direction of jazz in America remain obscure.

My intention here is not to provide a comprehensive history about each artist or to enumerate a list of facts and dates. My objective is to offer my personal experience with their art and acknowledge the Italian contribution to American Jazz.

Ted Fiorito

I have a special place for Ted Fiorito because of the namesake I share with him. I'm not going to lie and say that I searched him out because my dad talked about him when I was a kid. Surprisingly, the only time in my life people recognized the Fiorito name was when I worked on a retail floor in Berkeley, California just after college. WW2 retirees would look at my name tag and ask me if I was related to Ted Fiorito, the bandleader whose music piped out on the Army Broadcasts across the world. I went out to Berkeley to discover myself, to escape the world I grew up in, and there I was running smack into the old New York of my father's childhood.

Only many years later, at about 40 years old, I found a collection of Ted Fiorito music, "Spotlight on Ted Fiorito," on CD. I then later found another collection, "Never Been Blue." Here and there I've picked up singles like "When The Lights Go On Again," a song about soldiers returning from war, about life returning to normal after WW2.

From Ted Fiorito I became more interested in 20s music. I discovered other big bands of that era like Paul Whiteman, Ted Weems and Ben Pollack. I began to love the stylized pre-Sinatra falsetto voices of Russ Columbo and Nick Lucas. I became fascinated by the arrangements, bands playing without drums, using horseshoe clucks for percussion and tubas to hold down a bass line. I also fell in love with the vibraphone. You'll hear the vibraphone sometimes coming in at the end of a musical stop, capping off the stop with a bell tone ring.

Fiorito played in numerous big bands and other configurations. He joined Nick Lucas in a group called The Kentucky Five in about 1915, a band consisting mainly of New Jersey Italian-Americans.

Although Al Jolson became synonymous with "Toot Tootsie," it was written by Ted Fiorito. Some sources even show Jolson as having written it. But the fame Ted Fiorito gained from the success of "Tootsie" coincided with his co-leading a band with Dan Russo, who was already an established bandleader. From there he played in numerous incarnations with Dan Russo until he formed his own orchestra. He then recorded songs like "Simple And Sweet," "I'll Take An Option On You," "Soothing," "I'll String Along With You," and countless others.

In the 30s, Fiorito teamed with the "Debutantes" vocal trio and brought in guitarist Muzzy Marcellino and bassist Candy Candido, both of whom would become equally known for their vocals. Marcellino had an unusually clear and melodious whistle. His whistling was featured on Mickey Mouse and Lassie, and even The Good, The Bad and The Ugly soundtracks. Marcellino was also the uncle of Vincent Guaraldi, the pianist and songwriter associated with the music of "Peanuts." Candy Candido, born in New Orleans, provided unusual voices in films like Abbot and Costello in the Foreign Legion and others. Even Betty Grable briefly joined Fiorito's band. Though she didn't make any recordings with Fiorito, she appeared as a vocalist in the 1933 film "The Sweetheart of Sigma Chi."

At the peak of his popularity, Fiorito managed to succeed as a composer and bandleader and performed his songs in film.

Towards the end of his career, Fiorito moved to Scottsdale, Arizona, where he opened the Black Sheep Club. He continued to play in California and Nevada in different band incarnations until his death in 1971.

Adrian Rollini

Ask the first ten people you know who consider themselves music experts if they've ever heard of Adrian Rollini.

Rollini was a hub for music in the 20s and 30s, playing with Annette Hanshaw, Cliff Edwards (Ukelele Ike), Frank Signorelli, Joe Venuti and his Blue Four, Miff Mole, Red Nichols, Bix Beiderbecke, Frank Trumbauer and many others. Read the personnel listings on recordings from the 20s and 30s; you'll see Rollini's name often appearing. In fact, Rollini, Lang, Signorelli, Venuti, Trumbauer, and Bix played in many of the same configurations.

Born in Larchmont, New York in 1903, Rollini was considered a child prodigy. He was dubbed Professor Adrian Rollini at age 4, playing Chopin's Minute Waltz at the Waldorf Astoria Hotel. He played piano, bass saxophone, chimes and vibraphone, all extremely well. I don't see him credited for playing piano on recordings. He was credited for bass saxophone and vibraphone. The bass saxophone is an unusual instrument; I'm not exactly sure why anyone would want to learn it, except for the fact that it's so novel. It's difficult to even hold, much less play. The bass saxophone was more commonly used in orchestral music giving richness and depth to brass harmony arrangements.

Rollini also became an early master of the vibraphone, where he played behind many prominent jazz musicians, some already mentioned. Initially recognized for its novelty effects, vibraphone was then added to the arsenal of percussion sounds used by vaudeville orchestras. The vibraphone soon became a jazz instrument standardly employed for its dreamy percussive ring. Unlike its cousin the xylophone, the vibraphone is not a solo instrument. As only he could, Rollini wrote "Vibrolinni," a completely untypical composition for the instrument. The vibraphone provides atmosphere and color, but doesn't stand out as a featured jazz instrument. Despite this, Rollini pushed his playing of the vibraphone into exciting new directions.

In addition to playing as a sideman on notable artists' records, I have a collection of Rollini 1934-1938 recordings that has songs like "Davenport Blues," "Bouncin' In Rhythm," "Honeysuckle Rose," and others. It's a good collection but doesn't give you the depth and breadth of the man's great career. Rollini is the gem hidden in the songs of the 20s and 30s.

Nick Lucas

When I play Nick Lucas for people, often their first reaction is a chuckle. His choice of songs, though once standards, now sound corny and old fashioned. Also, he sings in a stylized falsetto like many pre-Sinatra popular vocalists of his time. The Nick Lucas collection I have is mainly solo works on guitar and vocals with songs like "Tiptoe Through the Tulips." Accompanying himself on guitar he can stand in front of the audience, making the guitar more intimate than the piano. His chord progressions are innovative and dynamic, giving the guitar the power to front an orchestra. Using the jump rhythms of jazz guitar, he also picks out the melodies to compliment his vocals. A guitar player can tell that he learned banjo before the guitar by the way he alternates his index and forefinger while using his thumb to maintain tempo. This ragtime style would be one of the branches of guitar evolution which would further develop in the hands of guitarists like Merle Travis and Chet Atkins.

Born Dominic Nicholas Anthony Lucanese in 1897 in New Jersey, he later changed his name legally to Nick Lucas. Nick's older brother Frank taught him music without any instrument using the solfeggio system. The idea behind solfeggio is that you first learn to sing a song before you play it on an instrument. This very Italian form of musical education has had a tremendous impact on Italians in music, particularly Italian-Americans. By never forgetting the melody, a musician can express the story of a song in instrumentation. A violin can weep, a guitar can gurgle like a brook, and a banjo can dance. Once Lucas mastered the solfeggio system, he then learned how to play the guitar, mandolin and banjo all while still very young.

According to Lucas, his brother Frank dragged him along to play at Italian christenings and weddings. "We even played on street corners and in saloons and I'd pass the hat around. I was getting a lot of experience because the Italian people, when they get to feeling good, like to dance all night long, especially the tarantella. We played for hours and hours, and my wrists got very tired, but I was getting great practical experience that paid off years later."

Lucas switched from tenor banjo to guitar after playing with his brother. He even played in The Kentucky Five and in the Russo-Fiorito Orchestra in the early 20s. He became known as "The Crooning Troubadour."

After cutting a string of hits on the Brunswick Label, he was then signed by Warner Brothers to sing "Gold Diggers of Broadway." In this film he sang, "Painting The Clouds With Sunshine" and "Tiptoe Through The Tulips With Me." During "Tiptoe" the dancers actually weaved through red and yellow tulips as Nick sang. "Tiptoe Through The Tulips With Me" sold three million copies in its initial pressing as a record and has since sold five million copies.

Lucas has had a lasting impact on the guitar. Listening to it today, his guitar playing still sounds inventive. Lucas developed a whole new vocabulary for guitar accompaniment; his ideas are still being assimilated by guitarists.

Eddie Lang

Among those listening to Nick Lucas was Eddie Lang. Born Salvatore Massaro in 1902 in Philadelphia, PA, he is considered the Father of Jazz Guitar, though he may not be well known today except among specialists. You can see a performance of Eddie Lang and Ruth Etting on YouTube from their 1932 film "A Regular Trouper." His guitar playing is subtle and dancelike; he never gets in the way of a vocalist. He could offer a light touch, or dazzle with a thumping rhythm, moving with the changing dynamics of a vocalist. As such, vocalists often worked with Lang. In addition to Etting, Lang played with Bing Crosby, Bessie Smith and countless others. He was a vocalist's guitar player.

I have a collection of Eddie Lang's solo guitar works called "Jazz Guitar Virtuoso." As it comes through on my shuffle, hearing individual songs out of context, it can be hard to identify a song I haven't memorized. There are elements of jazz, Delta blues and even bluegrass in Lang's playing. In the mix of all of these American styles, Lang added perhaps a bit of Neapolitan romanticism. Lang could play anything.

You might say that Lang killed the banjo. After Lang demonstrated that the guitar could be sophisticated, the banjo slowly disappeared from jazz orchestras. The advent of the electric recording for the guitar allowed it to develop a wide range of guitar sounds, from honking brass tones to rounder, softer accompaniment. Lang set the direction for what jazz guitar could be. Django Reinhardt, Les Paul and Charlie Christianson all benefited from Lang's trailblazing chording techniques.

Unsurprisingly, Lang initially played violin, taking lessons for 11 years. In school he became friends with Joe Venuti, who was a lifelong collaborator. By 1918, he was playing violin, banjo, and guitar professionally. He worked with various bands in the US, briefly played in London, then settled in New York City.

On February 4, 1927, Lang was featured in the recording of "Singin' the Blues" by Frankie Trumbauer and His Orchestra with Bix Beiderbecke on cornet. He was in the center of the storm.

In 1929, while with the Paul Whiteman Orchestra, Lang was introduced to Bing Crosby who was then an up-and-coming vocalist. They developed a close personal relationship which would propel Lang's career.

When Crosby signed a five-picture deal with Paramount Studios, he insisted Lang share the experience with him. Lang, playing guitar accompaniment, appeared with Crosby in their 1932 Hollywood feature film "The Big Broadcast."

Like Rollini, Lang played with numerous artists through his brief career. He is the quintessential jazz guitar player of the 20s and 30s.

Louis Prima

I remember as a kid dancing to "Buona Sera," "Please Don't Squeeze the Banana," and "Just A Gigolo." My mom had a Prima Greatest Hits record that we would go crazy listening to when all of the company left after Christmas.

For most of my life, Prima was a clowning musician who made some funny music. I didn't know how good a trumpet player he was or anything about his history.

Then I started to dig and learn more and more about his history and his music. I read a book called "Louis Prima" by Gary Boulard and learned Prima's dirty little secret. Because Sicilians weren't considered to be white, the white establishment wasn't concerned if Sicilians lived and played among blacks in New Orleans. So Prima and many other New Orleans Sicilians played in the homes, streets and bars of Storyville, learning the jazz idiom. The Italians in Storyville also brought their language and humor to the music. Prima combined his Sicilian dialect with rhythms and harmonies of jazz to make songs like "Please Don't Squeeze The Banana," "Angelina," "Buona Sera," and others. His music allowed for a private joke among the growing Italian-American population in America. They knew the lyrics were slightly off-color. They understood that when Prima sang "Zooma, Zooma Baccala" he wasn't referring to fishing. But most of all, the songs were entertaining. Prima had to change with the times, performing in smaller ensembles before the war, then playing in big bands, then playing in smaller ensembles again. The musicians and arrangements were tight, combining the dizzying rhythms and time signatures of New Orleans with comedy and theater.

Sharkey Bonano

Arturo Toscanini heard Sharkey in New York then hired him to come to a rehearsal of the New York Philharmonic to play a few solo numbers for his orchestra. After Sharkey played, Toscanini berated his trumpet section at length because they couldn't blow tones out of their instruments like Bonano.

Also known as Sharkey Banana or Sharkey Bananas, he was a jazz trumpeter, band leader and vocalist.

Joseph "Sharkey" Bonano was born in the Milneberg section of New Orleans in 1904. Milneberg had scores of cabarets on the boardwalk overlooking the water. Here, white and black jazz musicians listened and stole each other's performance styles and ideas.

Bonano played left handed like Nick LaRocca. He amused his audiences with his shimmy dances and comical routines. Out of the many white New Orleans jazz musicians like Leon Roppolo, Tony Parenti, and Santo Pecora, Sharkey distinguished himself with his terrific tone and entertaining style.

Riding out the Depression playing in small clubs around New Orleans, Bonano finally landed a residency at Prima's Penthouse. When Prima's Penthouse folded, he was lucky enough to attract the attention of a Greenwich Village tavern owner, Nick Rongetti.

Bonano wrote a number of classic tunes like "Yes She Do-No She Don't," "I'm Satisfied with My Gal," and "Wash It Clean." He also recorded popular songs of the day like "When You're Smiling," "Panama," and countless others.

At the end of his career, Bonano returned to his home town, New Orleans. He became a wildly successful tourist attraction. In some respects he was at the height of his career at this point, well established in New Orleans jazz history. He never stopped his shimmying and strutting until the end.

Wingy Manone

"Rhythm is Our Business" is the quintessential statement for Italians in New Orleans. Rhythm, virtuosity, style and theater describe the Italian-American contribution to jazz as typified by Wingy.

Wingy was born in New Orleans in 1900. Like Prima, he was a dazzling trumpet player, often interspersing patter with virtuosic trumpet leads. Unlike Prima, he frequently played as a sideman on recording sessions, though he also performed as a bandleader.

At the age of ten, he lost his arm in a street car accident. Afterwards, he was cruelly called "Wingy" by the people he knew. Playing the trumpet with one arm, Wingy broke his teeth playing on Mississippi River Boats. He then moved on, playing in New York, St. Louis and Chicago.

Like Prima and Bonano, Wingy was a highly skilled musician who entertained his audiences. Just listening to his recordings "Wingy Manone and His Orchestra 1935-1936," and

"Wingy Manone and His Orchestra 1944," you hear the comic vocal style and humorous lyrics.

For many years, Joe Venuti sent Wingy a single cuff-link on his birthday as a practical joke.

Leon Roppolo

When you listen to the early classic recordings of the New Orleans Rhythm Kings, you hear the searing melodic solos of Leon Roppolo's clarinet emerging from the fray of Dixeland band sounds. I personally find it magical that you can connect with 100 year old sounds recorded on poor quality technology, and without the benefit of modern recording techniques. Roppolo's clarinet rises like heat from the records. An ear that is not listening will not hear the powerful artistic genius of his clarinet. Someone who is listening will hear the brilliant high notes and the sheer energy projected across time, pushed out with explosive urgency. You can imagine Roppolo standing in front of a microphone twisting and contorting, playing with all of the intensity of a live performance. Recording was a relatively new art. Who knew how to arrange instruments and solos in the recording industry? "Make it sound live, give energy and vibrancy," is probably the direction the players were given.

Leon Roppolo was born March 16, 1901. Best known for his playing with the New Orleans Rhythm Kings, Roppolo also played saxophone and guitar.

Leon Joseph Roppolo was born in Lutcher, Louisiana near New Orleans. His family of Sicilian origin moved to the Uptown neighborhood of New Orleans about 1912. Roppolo first learned music playing the violin. This is a very common Italian-American phenomenon: bringing classical training and tonality into jazz. He was a fan of the Italian and non-Italian marching bands he heard in the streets of New Orleans and, as such, identified strongly with the clarinet.

Bringing the knowledge of music he developed from violin, Roppolo soon excelled at the clarinet. He played with his childhood friends Paul Mares and George Brunies for parades, parties, and at Milneburg on the shores of Lake Pontchartrain. In his teens Roppolo decided to leave home to travel with the band of Bee Palmer, which soon became the nucleus for the New Orleans Rhythm Kings. The Rhythm Kings became (along with King Oliver's band) one of the best regarded hot jazz bands in Chicago in the early 1920s. Many considered Roppolo to be the star. His style influenced many younger Chicago musicians, most famously Benny Goodman. Some critics have called Roppolo's work on the Rhythm Kings Gennett Records, the first recorded jazz solos.

After the breakup of the Rhythm Kings in Chicago, Roppolo and Paul Mares headed east to try their luck on the New York City jazz scene. Contemporary musicians recalled Roppolo making some recordings with Original Memphis Five and California Ramblers musicians in New York in 1924. These sides were presumably unissued, or if issued, unidentified.

Roppolo and Mares then returned home to New Orleans where they briefly reformed the Rhythm Kings and made some more recordings. After this, Roppolo worked with other New Orleans bands such as the Halfway House Orchestra, with which he recorded on saxophone.

In his later life, Roppolo, looking old and feeble far beyond his age, would come home for periods when a relative or friend could look after him and he would sit in with local bands on saxophone or clarinet.

Frank Signorelli

Frank Sinatra sings a version of Frank Signorelli's "I'll Never Be The Same" that goes right into your soul. The melody hooks into your head. Eddie Lang recorded a guitar version of it capturing a different mood of the melody. In Lang's hands it's less melancholy and more playful. Signorelli also wrote "Stairway to the Stars," and "A Blues Serenade" in the '30s. Sadly he was otherwise scarcely recorded.

Frank Signorelli was born in 1901 in New York City. Like many of the musicians in this review, Signorelli was an important player behind the scenes and an accompanying pianist with several notable bands. Many of these musicians played in the same ensembles and backed bigger named artists on countless records. Signorelli appeared on many classic records with Bix Beiderbecke, Frankie Trumbauer, Joe Venuti, and Eddie Lang during the era, plus on a countless number of recordings with dance bands and backing commercial singers. In 1917, with Phil Napoleon, he was a founding member of the Original Memphis Five. Signorelli was briefly a member of the Original Dixieland Jazz Band in 1921. In 1927, he was in Adrian Rollini's legendary New Yorker group. He played with a newer version of the Original Dixieland Jazz Band (1936-1938), worked with Paul Whiteman for a few months in 1938, and played regularly during the '40s and '50s (including at Nick's with Bobby Hackett) and helped organize the revived Original Memphis Five.

Despite this list of players and memories, I have to make room for new music. I play many of the musicians and singers I've listed here for my sons, but they prefer their own music, like rap and hip-hop. And I try to listen and learn. Keeping the music on at most times will likely make the melodies and memories alike stick in their minds.

All or Nothing at All

When I was a kid, my father talked about how Jimmy Roselli sang in the real Neapolitan dialect, unlike Jerry Vale, who appealed to a more American audience. In Neapolitan dialect, Napoli becomes Napule and Sorrento becomes Surriento. The funny thing is that my father didn't even understand Neapolitan. He might have known a few words, but like most Italian-Americans his age, he didn't grow up speaking Italian.

Years after my father died, I read about Roselli and the Canzone Napoletana tradition. I was inspired to visit the one place where Canzone Napoletana still lives, E. Rossi & Company, at the corner of Mulberry and Grand in New York's Little Italy.

E. Rossi & Co sells *articoli Italiani* — Italian goods: Neapolitan coffee pots, spaghetti makers, clothes, and religious statues and icons. Rossi's had originally been a publishing house; they published Neapolitan songs and sold the records, too. E. Rossi & Co has a unique catalog of sheet music that cannot be found anywhere else in the world, but these days it looks more like an Italian five-and-dime store.

Having grown up in New York City, I had known the store all of my life. I just didn't know the history and importance of E. Rossi & Co. I only knew what you could see through the window; the trinkets and the kitchenware.

Even though it was only a few subway stops away, I called before I went down to the store and spoke to Ernie, the grandson of the original owner. Ernie was immediately friendly and talkative on the phone.

"Are you related to Ted Fiorito?" Ernie asked when I told him my name. He was referring to the famous bandleader and composer from the 1930s and '40s. I said that I wasn't. "You should tell people you are!" he said, jokingly.

When I walked into the store, I found Ernie sitting on a stool behind the counter. From where he sat he could work the cash register, pull down CDs from the rack, and show statues of holy saints on the shelves. Ernie was a portly man with a gentle face. He was about sixty. He had a healthy head of messy gray hair and wore reading glasses.

"I'm the guy who called earlier," I said.

Ernie smiled and we shook hands. In the piles of spaghetti strainers and bread slicers stacked up behind the counter, I spotted a guitar.

"I see you play guitar," I said. He nodded. "I do too," I said.

While we talked, people in the store interrupted to ask prices for espresso pots, a soccer ball decked out with Italy's national colors, a jacket embroidered with a map of Italy — the renowned boot.

I asked him to show me his Jimmy Roselli CDs. "Jimmy used to come here to drop off his CDs for the store," said Ernie. "He brings them himself and looks around for sheet music."

Reaching into a stack of CDs, Ernie pulled one out and popped it into the player. Roselli's "Torna a Surriento" filled the store. I knew the song because my father had often sung the opening lines: *"Vide 'o mare quant'è bello; spira tantu sentiment."* See how beautiful the sea is; it inspires immense feeling in me.

Ernie handed me the CD cover. It had a picture of a woman playing a guitar, like a vintage label on a can of tomato sauce. He cranked up the volume, and Roselli sang like he'd been stabbed in the heart and could no longer breathe. Everyone in the store looked up when Roselli's voice rang out, as if it was thundering from heaven. From God. Ernie didn't seem to care that the music was very loud. When he turned the music off, the blast of explosive sound was swallowed by a sudden silence.

I asked Ernie what kind of music he played on guitar. He then reached behind the counter, pulled out his guitar, and said, "I'm going to sing you a song now."

A woman approached the counter to purchase a few items: a pair of cheap slippers, a framed picture of the pope, a few red-white-green Italian boot magnets. As she thrust them towards the counter to pay, Ernie waved her away with a hand.

"Now I play a song. You pay later," he said.

He started strumming. As he sang, the first few notes were loud and slightly out of key, but his voice was strong. His voice got louder and steadier with each word. His face twisted, his mouth curved to one side when he sang. He sang with heart, like he was crying.

I turned to look at the woman who earlier had told us she was a tourist from Austria. She stood near the counter holding the slippers, tears running down her cheeks. She was wiping the tears with a tissue. It felt strange to stand next to her, helplessly, while she cried. Seeing her response to the song made me flush with emotion, too.

When Ernie finished, everyone clapped enthusiastically. He put his guitar down and sat behind the register again. The Austrian woman had now dried her tears, so she stacked her items on the counter to pay for them.

After she'd left, Ernie asked, "What happened to that woman?"

"You made her cry," I said, thinking that she must have felt the same pang in her gut as I had. "Maybe your song reminded her of someone; maybe she was married to an Italian, or her father or grandfather was Italian," I added. La Canzone Napoletana pulls at your heart strings.

When I visit my mother, I often talk to her about music and play songs for her. My mother has always been strong-willed and in control of her emotions. I once played Pavarotti singing Neapolitan songs for her. She said that she'd grown up listening to those same songs.

"When I hear that music, it hits me right here," she said, pointing to her heart. I could see that her eyes were wet with emotion.

I keep a guitar at my mother's apartment to play when I visit. Sometimes I'll play a few songs for her. She's a tough audience. She looks at me over her reading glasses. This makes her eyes look bigger. I feel like I'm performing for an instructor at Julliard. If I can play for my mom, I can play for anyone.

One time, I played a traditional British Isles tune that had taken a long time to learn. The song is called "Martinmas Mass," also known as "South Wind." When I finished, I looked up. I was proud that I could finally play the song from beginning to end, and in front of someone.

"What did you think?" I asked.

"I was waiting for you to do something?" she said.

"What do you mean?"

"You played it nicely. It's a pretty song. But it's like, nothing happens," she shrugged.

After I recovered from that comment, I realized that she was absolutely right. Unlike the song I played, the Neapolitan song tradition is dramatic. It is sung like the singer is on fire, like life or death is on the line. There is no middling. It's all or nothing at all. Reflecting the desperation of the region the songs came from, it is a song tradition associated with ebullience, melancholy, joy, and fatalism — all wrapped together.

Many of the songs deal with being far away from a loved one, *lontano*. There is often the mention of *lacreme*, or tears. There are remembrances of the beautiful Southern Italian landscape, of flowers and sunshine. These songs were written by and for Southern Italians who, from about 1880 to 1920, had fled poverty and oppression in their own country and now lived in distant places, like Canada, the United States, and Australia. Although they could never return to their home country to make a living, they could fantasize about it.

The Neapolitan song is typically sung in the bel canto style, which originated from Italian opera. Bel canto focuses on breath control, resonation, and natural approach. It emphasizes story telling. It's vulnerable, but it's strong.

Many of the Neapolitan songs are world-famous because they were carried to new countries by emigrants from Naples and Southern Italy. The music was also popularized abroad by Enrico Caruso, who took to singing the popular music of his native city in his encores at New York's Metropolitan Opera in the early 1900s. Caruso is responsible for the fact that operatic tenors since then have been required to know these songs.

While the Southern Italians brought their vitality and strong bodies to work in the countries they adopted, they also brought their musical traditions, their dreams, and their longings. The American music industry can be traced back to Caruso. He was one of the first recorded vocalists, and his records sold wildly. It can be said that Caruso's rock star success and fame launched the music industry as we know it today.

Caruso also popularized the bel canto style. Bel canto's long, elegantly phrased notes allow the vocalist to be expressive and to tell a story. You can draw a line from the Italian Romantic songs of Rossini and Bellini sung by Caruso to Sinatra. This legato singing style even found its way into jazz. I once heard that when asked how to interpret a particular jazz standard tune, Miles Davis told John Coltrane to play it "like Sinatra sings."

As Mark Rotella wrote in his book, <u>Amore: The Story of Italian American Song</u> [New York: Farrar, Strauss, & Giroux. 2010], bel canto was passed on from Sinatra to Motown and became the singing style most associated with American music. Bel canto is warm, it's vulnerable and invites the listener in to hear the story behind the words. Along with building railroads, bridges, and highways, Southern Italians changed the world through song.

What follows is a list of resources about the Neapolitan Song tradition, along with links to, what I consider to be, definitive versions of the songs.

Epilogue

As I revisit these stories, I know that the world I grew up in has nearly vanished. And that's okay. My sons, Theo and Travis, have to sometimes bear the music I play for them. They mostly tolerate what I put on. But the fact is, the world has moved on. Italian-American neighborhoods are a thing of the past. And while there is a lingering bias towards Italian-Americans, Italians have become part of American culture – even if it's to be mimicked in insulting ways. But what I leave my sons and the generations that follow is the music. Along with the love that I try desperately to pass on, the affection, the kindness, I am hoping the music will ring in their ears with each memory of an embrace.

Appendix

All links can be found as published by Ovunque Siamo online at:

https://ovunquesiamoweb.wordpress.com/current-issue-vol-l-issue-6/mike-fiorito/

Films Online

Closing Time

A number of years ago, E. Rossi & Co was forced to move out of the location they had been in for a hundred years. The film Closing Time was made by an Italian woman from Rome who was visiting the United States and was so struck by E. Rossi & Co's story that she dropped everything and made a short film on the spot. The documentary is available online at http://www.folkstreams.net/

The Neapolitan Heart

Another wonderful film that outlines the history of Neapolitan Song is The Neapolitan Heart. There are performances by singers from Naples, as well as an interview with Jimmy Roselli. The Neapolitan Heart is available on YouTube.

Some Neapolitan Songs and Vocalists

"Core 'ngrato"

There are many versions of "Core 'ngrato," but my favorite is by Giuseppe di Stefano. He sings it with the reckless abandon of a defeated lover. You can hear the wretched sadness in his voice when he chokes, singing that his lover doesn't remember him anymore.

Enrico Caruso sings great versions of all of these songs. His delivery is something of a high wire act; we're never sure if he's going to be able to hit the high note, or come careening off a passage to land in the right place. But he does. Sadly, however, the recordings aren't crisp. Some remixes have isolated his stunning voice, but the instruments behind him sound like bicycle horns. "Core 'ngrato" (Ungrateful Heart) was written in 1911 by Salvatore Cardillo, an Italian composer who had recently emigrated to the United States, with lyrics by Riccardo Cordiferro (real name Alessandro Sisca). It was adopted by Enrico Caruso but it is not known whether he commissioned Cardillo and Sisca to write it. It is the only well-known standard Neapolitan song to have been written in America. The song's title comes from the heartfelt passage, "Core, core 'ngrato, te haie pigliato 'a vita mia! Tutt' è passato, e nun nce pienze cchiù!" Ungrateful heart, you have stolen my life! It's all over and I don't think about it anymore!

"A Cartulina e Napule"

Published by E. Rossi & Co, "A Cartulina e Napule" (A Postcard from Naples), sung by Giulietta Sacco, is a song about longing for Naples and the Southern Italian diaspora. With tears in her eyes, the singer tells us how she misses Naples from her new home in America. This would have resonated very strongly with the newly arrived Italian immigrants.

"Malafemmena"

Jimmy Roselli recorded many of the Neapolitan songs and also sings variations of them. His version of "Malafemmena" is one of my favorites.

I also like Mina Mazzini's version. Whereas Roselli's is like a man riding a bull, hers is slow and delicate. Mina is a soprano known for her range of three octaves. A pop singer in her early years in the 1970s, Mina has always possessed the power and drama of the Neapolitan song. Louis Armstrong famously declared her to be "the greatest white singer in the world." Songs like "Se Telefonando," with music and arrangement by Ennio Morricone, are powerful masterpieces. "Se Telefonadano" builds dramatically through escalating tonal transitions. Mina's voice soars through Morricone's sophisticated arrangement of melodic trumpet lines. Mina has since performed other songs, like "Core 'Ngrato," "Maruzzella," and "Aggio Perduto Suonno," in the Neapolitan tradition.

"Malafemmena" was written by the Neapolitan actor Totò (Antonio de Curtis) in 1951. It has become one of the most popular Italian songs, a classic of the canzone Napoletana genre, and has been recorded by many artists.

"O Sole Mio"

Luciano Pavarotti sings a heart-shattering rendition of this song, which will make your eyes overflow with tears.

Of course, many others have sung it well, too. "'O Sole Mio" (My Sunshine) was written in 1898. Its lyrics were written by Giovanni Capurro and the music was composed by Eduardo di Capua and Alfredo Mazzucchi. There are other versions of "'O Sole Mio" but it is usually sung in the original Neapolitan language. "'O Sole Mio" is the Neapolitan equivalent of standard Italian il mio sole.

"'O Surdato 'nnammurato"

"'O Surdato 'nnammurato" (The Soldier in Love) is a famous song written in the Neapolitan language. The words were written by Aniello Califano and the music composed by Enrico Cannio in 1915. The song describes the sadness of a soldier who is fighting at the front lines during World War I, and who pines for his beloved.

"o' Marenariello"

Like so many of these songs, there are several terrific versions of "O' Marenariello" (The Tiny Sailor). This is because the melodies are lush and romantic, and they allow the singer to embellish the vocal lines with fioritura. Pavarotti delivers a towering version of "O' Marenariello." Sergio Bruni's version is more pensive, but powerful, too. The version most Americans know is by

Vito Rocco Farinola, or Vic Damone, as he is better known, and is entitled "I Have But One Heart."

"O' Marenariello" was written in 1893 by Salvatore Gambardella with lyrics by Gennaro Ottaviano.

"Torna a Surriento"

Once again, there are many great versions of this song. However, Jimmy Roselli sings it like a man filling the Neapolitan valleys with his enormous voice.

"Torna a Surriento" was composed in 1902 by Italian musician Ernesto De Curtis to words by his brother, the poet and painter Giambattista De Curtis. The song was copyrighted officially in 1905, and has since become one of the most popular Neapolitan songs, along with other hits in the genre, such as "O Sole Mio," "Funiculi Funicula" and "Santa Lucia." De Curtis wrote a number of Neapolitan songs: "Voce 'e Notte," "Non ti Scordar di Me," "Ti Voglio Tanto Bene," and many others.

"Piscatore 'e Pusilleco"

Claudia Villa sings an impassioned version of this song. Villa sings, "Piscatò, 'sti parole sò llacreme" (Fisherman, these words are my tears), and we believe every word. The tears pour right into our own hearts. "Piscatore 'e Pusilleco" was written in 1925, with music by Ernesto Tagliaferri and lyrics by Roberto Murolo. Murolo was an important composer, performer, and scholar of Neapolitan song.

"Primo Amore"

"Primo Amore" (First Love) by Carlo Buti can only be described as heavenly. Buti was born in Florence, but, in part due to Caruso's influence on Italian singers, he had to sing some of the Neapolitan canon. His unique warm and melodic tenorino style of high quasi-falsetto phrasing sung in the mezza voce makes his voice quiver like a violin bow.

"Aneme e' Core"

"Aneme e Core" (Soul and Heart), as sung by Connie Francis, is like listening to bright sunshine. Unlike the torrent of storms that Neapolitan songs evoke, her renditions are calming and peaceful. Connie Francis was born Concetta Rosa Maria Franconero in Brooklyn in 1937, and her career remains active to this day.

There are also versions of "Anema e Core" recorded by Pier Angeli, Jimmy Roselli, and Roberto Murolo that are terrific, each in their own way. The song was first introduced in 1950, sung by the opera tenor Tito Schipa. The composer was Salve d'Esposito, and the original lyrics were written by Tito Manlio.

Acknowledgements

While this book is yet so small, there are still many people to thank for bringing it into the world.

Thanks to Mad Swirl, Narratively, Chagrin River Review, and The Honest Ulsterman for publishing earlier versions of some of these stories.

Thank you to Susan Kaessinger and Bill Bern for providing multiple reviews and proofs.

And thank you to Paul Paolicelli, John Keahey, Alfonso Colasuonno, Joey Nicoletti, Jennifer Coella Maretelli, and Louisa Calio for your support.

And thank you to Michelle Messina Reale and the staff at Ovunque Siamo for believing in me and giving Call Me Guido a proper home. I've written a number of these pieces for Ovunque Siamo so it's very fitting that they are now being published by its magazine press. Michelle has created a community for Italian-American literature and studies that will permanently change its course.

Thank you to my wife, Arielle, for her insights into all of my work. Your patience and openness help make all of this possible.

And finally, thank you to my family for always being there and for teaching me how to love.

About the author

Call Me Guido is Mike Fiorito's third book. His short story collections Freud's Haberdashery Habits & Other Stories and Hallucinating Huxley were published by Alien Buddha Press. Mike's writings have appeared in Ovunque Siamo, Narratively, Mad Swirl, Pif Magazine, Longshot Island, Beautiful Losers, The Honest Ulsterman, Chagrin River Review, The New Engagement and many other publications. Mike is an Associate Editor for Mad Swirl magazine. He has been nominated for a Pushcart Prize.

For more information please visit www.callmeguido.com or email callmeguido2@gmail.com

Made in the USA
Middletown, DE
25 May 2019